TOURNAMENT OF TERROR

Draco Falcon, fully armored and mounted on his Arab stallion, looked across the tournament field to where his opponent impatiently waited. Never before had Falcon gazed upon so awesome a foe as Rollo Dupre, a giant astride a steed as larger-than-life as he.

Already Draco had seen Dupre turn this tournament into a bloodbath as knight after knight fell before his incredible strength and infinite savagery. Already Draco was steeling himself for the charge to come. And for the first time in his fighting life, Draco Falcon faced the vivid specter of one-on-one defeat in the form of a champion of evil as powerful and pitiless as death itself. . . .

More SIGNET Action-Adventure Series

(0451)

☐ **BEAT A DISTANT DRUM (American Avenger #1)** by Robert Emmett. (112679—$2.50)*

☐ **RIDE THE TIGER (American Avenger #2)** by Robert Emmett. (112687—$2.50)*

☐ **THE DEVIL'S FINGER (American Avenger #3)** by Robert Emmett. (114582—$2.50)*

☐ **KING, BISHOP, KNIGHT (American Avenger #4)** by Robert Emmett. (116208—$2.50)*

☐ **TROJAN HORSES (American Avenger #5)** by Robert Emmett. (118251—$2.50)*

☐ **THE FALCON STRIKES (1st in the Falcon series)** by Mark Ramsay. (117700—$2.50)*

☐ **THE BLACK POPE (2nd in the Falcon series)** by Mark Ramsay. (117719—$2.50)*

☐ **THE BLOODY CROSS (3rd in the Falcon series)** by Mark Ramsay. (119177—$2.50)*

☐ **NIGHT AND FOG (Resistance #1)** by Gregory St. Germain. (118278—$2.50)*

☐ **MAGYAR MASSACRE (Resistance #2)** by Gregory St. Germain. (118286—$2.50)*

*Prices slightly higher in Canada

THE BLOODY CROSS

by

Mark Ramsay

Ⓞ

A SIGNET BOOK

NEW AMERICAN LIBRARY

TIMES MIRROR

The first chapter of this book appeared in *The Black Pope*,
the second volume of this series.

ONE

THE ROAD heading toward Paris was muddy. But then, it was fall, and roads leading everywhere were muddy. The two riders were cursing the mud, the rain, the slow pace of their mounts, and anything else that occurred to them.

"My mail's going to rust," said the younger rider. He wore a steel cap, beneath which hung a curtain of tangled yellow hair.

"Roll it up and stow it in an oiled bag, as I did with mine," said the elder. He was a striking man, tall and lean, with a blaze of white hair running in a streak through his otherwise coal-black locks.

"And ride unprotected through strange territory?" said the yellow-haired man. "You can pamper that fine Saracen gear of yours if you like, but I'm willing to put up with a little rust." He scanned the dripping trees. "That inn has to be somewhere near."

"Why?" grumbled the other. " 'About two hours

from here,' that peasant said. Two hours for what? A horse? A man? A peasant carrying a load of fire-wood?"

"If he was talking about two hours for an eagle, we're in trouble," the younger man said.

They rounded a bend. A short distance from them they could see a crossroads, and at the crossroads was a collection of low, rambling buildings. There were sheds and stables and a courtyard, all surrounded by a timber stockade. "The inn!" both men shouted at once. They kicked their horses into a trot.

As they rode up, they could see a cheery light coming from under the thatched eaves. They had been riding all day, and they dismounted somewhat stiffly. A boy came to take their horses, and they picked up their bags and went inside.

The innkeeper met them at the door. "Come in, sirs, and good day to you. You look hungry and cold and wet. Please make yourselves comfortable by the fire while I send for some refreshment for you. How shall I announce you?"

The men gave their names and followed the man into a low-beamed, smoky room. Gathered around a hearth were about twenty people from all stations in life. Some were eating, and all were drinking wine or ale.

The innkeeper said importantly: "My lords and ladies and others, I present Sir Draco Falcon and his man, Wulf." Those gathered made a place for the men near the fire and scanned Falcon surreptitiously. He was a tall man with handsome, hawklike features. His face was burned deep brown, bisected by a thin white line that began at his hairline at the base of the white streak and ran down through his eyebrow and down the cheek and jaw and neck to disappear beneath his tunic. The eyebrow was white where the line crossed it. The men and the women present were impressed with what they saw, though for different reasons.

A man handed Falcon a cup of hot spiced wine. "I am Philippe de Chambord, Sir Draco. I am master of the vintners' guild of Paris." Philippe wore clothing that was rich though travel-stained. The vintners' guild stood high in the royal favor. "We've just been discussing the latest news. Have you heard about Richard Lion-Heart of England?"

"Richard? No, I haven't heard about him in months."

"He's dead," said a man past middle age, attired as a knight. "The light of chivalry is dead at the siege of Chaluz."

"Dead?" Falcon said. It saddened him. He had hoped to kill Richard himself someday. "How? And where is Chaluz?"

"It's a castle belonging to the Viscount of Limoges," the old knight said. "He and Richard were embroiled in some petty affray over a treasure trove. They say that a crossbowman shot Richard in the neck. The wound was not serious, but it festered and he died."

"A crossbowman? Richard? How fitting!" Falcon could not help chuckling, though some of those present were scandalized. It was known throughout Christendom that Richard had shocked the world by wielding a crossbow in the Crusade. The weapon had been forbidden for use against Christians, but the Pope had declared it lawful for killing heathens. Still, the sight of a king using a weapon relegated to the lowest of footmen had shaken the world of chivalry.

Falcon removed his sword belt and seated himself on a stool, holding the sword propped between his knees. It was long and curved, clearly not of European origin. Its guard was a bronze crescent and its haft was long enough for two hands. The pommel was a smaller crescent.

The innkeeper's servants brought Falcon a platter of bread and cheeses and sausages, and he began to eat ravenously.

"Sir Draco," said a lady seated nearby, "may I refill your cup?" The lady stood and brought him a pitcher of wine. He placed her accent somewhere near the Rhine. She was unusually tall, close to six feet, and her tight-fitting gown revealed that she was built with a Junoesque lushness. Her coif and wimple hid her hair, but her eyebrows were so white as to be nearly invisible. Her features were large, regular, and handsome rather than conventionally beautiful. "I am Lady Gudrun von Kleist. I am returning from a pilgrimage to Rome."

"By way of Paris?" Falcon asked.

"I've always wanted to see Paris," Lady Gudrun said.

Whatever for, Falcon wondered. "Do you travel alone or in company?" he asked. Ordinarily pilgrims were safe upon the roads, even women on pilgrimage alone, but the times were troubled and many brigands and robber barons regarded even pilgrims as fair game.

"I have my ladies with me, and a cook and groom, and a few pages and such. Aside from these, I am alone." It was clear that Lady Gudrun regarded herself as in company only with persons of her own rank. "Oh," she continued, "there is also Fra Benedetto." She gestured toward a seated man who wore the habit of a friar. Within his raised cowl, the obscured head bowed slightly. Falcon bowed slightly in return. Very slightly. He was not fond of the church, nor of its minions. At an early age, his boyish religious enthusiasms had been washed away in the bloodbaths of the Crusades. Once upon a time, he had been shocked deeply at the corruption and venality of the church. Now he was not even amused.

Fra Benedetto was attired as a Franciscan, but his habit, while of the order's plain design and cut, was of fine cloth. The man raised delicate white hands and pushed the cowl back, exposing a face small-boned and slightly vulpine. He smiled with thin lips. "Good evening, Sir Draco," he said. He spoke Provençal but his accent was thick Italian.

"Fra Benedetto," Lady Gudrun said, "has been kind enough to accompany us since we left Rome." Her expression and tone said that this kindness had been unwanted and unasked for. "Sir Draco," she continued, "I take it that Paris is your destination also?"

"It is, my lady."

"How wonderful! Will you consent to ride with us? With the roads so dangerous in these disgraceful times, the presence of armed men such as you and your squire would be a great comfort."

Falcon groaned inwardly. He had been fearing this. He hated to move with a pack of straggling foot travelers. He had been hoping to reach Paris within two days. Now he would be lucky to make it in six. There was no help for it, though. A knight was required to supply protection if asked by a lady of high birth.

"I am, of course, at my lady's disposal," Falcon said. Almost unconsciously, he had slipped into the courtly French of castle and palace. Ordinarily, he spoke the rough soldier's patois of the camps.

"Then I am sure we shall travel in safety," Lady Gudrun said, "with so chivalrous a gentleman riding before us." Falcon had little use for the artificial conventions of chivalry, but there was no escaping them. Within a generation, the vague rules of conduct for

5

warriors concocted by crusaders, poets, and priests had become the international rage of the military aristocracy. It had been further embroidered by court ladies weary of living with armored brutes of husbands until it was something as unreal as a fairy tale.

A sudden thought struck Falcon as he brooded in his winecup. "My God!" he exclaimed.

"What is it, sir?" asked the vintner.

"If Richard's dead, that means John Lackland's King of England. If King Philip wants to take England, there was never a better time." This remark caused a babble of comment.

Falcon's mind worked furiously. If King Philip, who was now being called Augustus, wanted to invade England, he would be hiring soldiers. Falcon was captain of a band of professionals who hired their services to the highest bidder. Until now, they had been fighting petty affrays, settling squabbles between barons over land or honor. Here was the prospect of a major campaign. If Philip took England from John, every one of Falcon's men could become rich. Falcon and his wellborn officers could expect to be made major landholders.

He had other reasons to hope for a war. If King Philip called up his vassals, Odo FitzRoy would have to appear with his men. In England, Falcon would find Nigel Edgehill among the opposing forces. He had sworn a holy oath to kill these two men, and two others. One of the four he had tracked down and killed two years before. Another, the Archbishop de Beaumont, he had found, but the man had escaped. Edgehill and FitzRoy he had not seen in more than a dozen years.

"I think not, just yet," said the vintner, interrupting Falcon's reverie.

"Why do you say that?" Falcon asked.

"Philip Augustus has enough troubles at home without indulging in military adventures abroad. Richard's death is a heaven-sent opportunity to take back all the lands seized by the Old King, but Philip is still deeply in debt for the funds he borrowed to mount his Crusade. My own guild alone has been owed ten thousand golden florins for more than ten years."

The Old King of whom the vintner spoke was Henry II of England, who had inherited, married, and conquered his way to the largest empire since the fall of Rome, most of it at the expense of the King of France. He had reduced Philip's father's holdings to a few acres of land around Paris, and Philip had spent the whole of his reign gradually reconquering his lost lands from Henry's valiant but foolish son, Richard.

"No," the vintner went on. "I think that now King Philip will go on consolidating his gains, and he will be successful now that he has no Richard to stop him. He will, of course, demand that John come to Paris to do homage for the crown of England. John will refuse, or delay, or pretend that he didn't get the demand, or just ignore it, and things will go on like that indefinitely, as each waits for the other to die first."

As hereditary dukes of Normandy, the Plantagenets supposedly held England in fief to the King of France, and had to renew their legitimacy with every generation by performing the oath of homage. This was legalistic fiction, for all the world knew that the Plantagenets held England by right of conquest and only needed to do homage for their French holdings, which until a few years before had included Normandy, Brittany, the Aquitaine, Anjou, and a dozen minor holdings. In short, about ninety percent of France. Richard had recklessly squandered his inheritance, and now England possessed only a few holdings along the English Channel. Falcon was sure that

Philip, ablest king of his line for many generations, would have those holdings back within a year.

He sighed. The vintner was probably right. It would have been a wonderful opportunity, though.

The next day, the motley band loaded up and set out for Paris. Falcon fretted impatiently as the group straggled out in the most inefficient fashion. His own little army would have been up before dawn and five miles down the road before the first of these travelers left the inn.

There were compensations to traveling with such a group, though. Several musicians had their instruments out and were leading the band in a rousing song. A juggler was keeping six balls in the air, bouncing one off his head from time to time. A tumbler was walking along in imitation of an old man, but his pack was strapped to his belly and his staff was gripped between his toes as he walked along on his hands. Falcon could not help smiling despite his impatience.

"Is the day not beautiful?" Lady Gudrun had ridden to Falcon's side. The lowering skies of the previous day had given way to clear autumn sunlight, and the puddles in the road lay steaming.

"Beautiful, indeed, my lady," Falcon acknowledged, openly admiring the German lady's graceful carriage. It was something few women could achieve riding sidesaddle. Today the lady wore a pink gown trimmed with ermine. It was so tightly fitted that Falcon could count every bone in her spearshaft-straight spine. He noted with interest that her large breasts bore uncommonly small nipples.

She noted, and reciprocated, his admiration. Besides his height, his handsome, aquiline features, and his striking coloration, she noted that his shoulders were wide, and that even dressed in mail his waist was as small as hers. His fine armor shimmered in the sunlight like quicksilver. The coif of mail hung down his back, to be drawn over his head at need. His conical helmet hung from his saddle next to an ax. On the other side was hung a long, kite-shaped shield. In his belt were a pair of thick gloves of black leather, their backs densely studded with small steel spikes. His soft boots were cross-gartered to the knee with strips of scarlet leather.

After a careful study of the man, masked by inconsequential talk, her attention was drawn to the device painted on his shield. In recent years, knights had taken to painting colored designs on the faces of their shields, to make themselves recognizable in battle. The practice had grown with the adoption of helms that covered the knight's face, and now it was part of the mystique of chivalry.

Falcon's device was a bird of prey, its wings spread against a white background. In its claws were clutched bolts of blue lightning. The bird was black. On Falcon's banner the background was embroidered in silver thread, but silver gilding was too expensive for something as perishable as a shield, so white had to do.

"Oh, now I see," Lady Gudrun said. "Your name is Falcon, and that is the name of the bird in your language, isn't it?"

"Yes, it is, my lady," Falcon said, sensing a ploy. The woman spoke French fluently, though she sometimes used an awkward Germanic construction. She couldn't have spent so much time in the courts of France without learning all the terms of falconry.

"You resemble your namesake," she said, "at least in appearance. Do you also resemble it in habit?"

9

"Somewhat. Like the bird, I seek game to feed my dependents."

"And have you a nest somewhere?"

"Wherever my men are."

"Ah. You serve no liege, then?"

"No, my lady. I'm a free captain. I hire my services and those of my army to any who need such. I am bound by no oath of fealty and I have no land. Just now, my men are in winter quarters in the South."

"And what brings you to Paris, so far from your men?"

Falcon smiled. The woman was pumping him for information without giving any in return. "There is a man there who desires my services. I'm going there to meet him. And you, my lady—Paris is not the finest of cities to visit. What draws you there?"

"Oh," Gudrun said, with an airy wave of her hand, "I've been invited to the court. King Philip desires closer ties with the Graf von Kleist."

"The graf is your husband?" Falcon asked.

"Oh, no!" she said. "The graf is my son. My husband died on Crusade and is with the saints in heaven. Little Klaus is only four years old. I hope to make a good marriage for him, perhaps even one of the royal princesses."

Falcon nodded. Gudrun was in the most enviable position possible for a noble lady. As mother of the heir, she could not be displaced, and she had control of her son's estates until he attained his majority, still many years in the future. As a young and beautiful widow of good blood, she had plenty of time to negotiate an advantageous marriage for herself before handing the reins over to her son. In the meantime, she was free to travel and amuse herself on her own, something most noble women could never hope to do. Ordinarily, a noble lady was regarded as little more than a brood mare, designed for the purpose of turning out children until she was used up and then being shunted aside in favor of a young mistress. Gudrun would never suffer that ignominy.

Their conversation was interrupted by the arrival of Fra Benedetto. Gudrun greeted him politely, but she wore a look of annoyance. The friar was riding an extremely fine palfrey, in violation of the rules of his order and of the sumptuary laws which regulated every facet of a person's life, down to the type of clothes he could wear, the breed of horse he could ride, and the type of hawk he could fly.

"You're well mounted, friar," Falcon said pointedly. He noted that the man's feet were covered by shoes of fine Cordoba leather, sewn with tiny seed pearls. Barefoot friars indeed! Falcon thought.

"I ride on the Holy Father's business," Benedetto said. "For this reason, I am spared the customary asceticism of my order. It is a long walk from Rome to Paris."

"Since when have Benedictine friars been acting as papal legates?" Falcon asked. The Franciscans, once the most devoted of ministers to the poor, had grown uncommonly lax of late.

"The Holy Father finds my particular skills of some use," Benedetto answered. "As a mendicant friar, I am under the authority of no abbot and thus I report only to the Throne of St. Peter. I am of sufficiently high birth to speak in the highest courts of Christendom, and I speak a number of languages. Let us say that, if not indispensable, I am at least not without value."

"For how much longer, I wonder?" Gudrun said. Falcon could not help smiling at the look of sour discomfiture that crossed the friar's face. The new Pope was Innocent III, and for the first time in generations a genuinely good, religious, and capable man wore the Fisherman's ring. He was engaged in a thorough housecleaning in Rome, and was purging the higher clergy of its worst elements. He was doing much to restore the tattered prestige of the papacy, but his influence was still unfelt here in France, and probably would not be for years.

"My lady," Benedetto began, "I am quite—"

His words were cut short by the appearance of a band of men on the road before them. There were at least twenty of them, and Falcon didn't like their look. Six were mounted, the rest on foot. The footmen were common outlaws. Most had lopped ears, branded foreheads, or lumps of scar where their noses had been: the marks of the public executioner. The mounted men wore helmets and rusty armor, but their spurs were of plain steel, denoting men who had been degraded from the status of knighthood.

"Stand where you are!" shouted one. "We want your goods and no more. Lay down your arms and pile everything you have in the road; then you can go freely." The bandits were eying Gudrun greedily.

"They're lying," Falcon said. "They'll take any who can be held for ransom prisoner and kill the rest."

"You must save us," Benedetto said.

"How?" retorted Gudrun.

Wulf rode up to Falcon and tossed him a twelve-foot lance with an ash shaft. The younger man readied his own weapons: a short curved sword and a small round shield. He studied the men before them.

"Too many, my lord," he said. "Too many even for you."

"I don't like bandits," Falcon said, glaring at the men.

"Who does? They are still too many. Let's get away from here while we can."

"You would not leave us?" Gudrun protested.

"The lady can come with us," Wulf said. "Her horse is a good one and she rides well. What use have we for a pack of townsmen? Let's go!"

Falcon never took his glare off the bandits. With a snarl he trotted his mount forward. Wulf sighed and followed his master. Falcon stopped about ten yards in front of the bandits.

"This group includes pilgrims and churchmen," Falcon said. "You risk excommunication."

The bandits merely laughed. "Do you think we fear that?" said one. Falcon had not expected them to.

He was too close to charge, and all the men held their shields low. Without warning, he raised the lance and cast it like a javelin at one of the horsemen. Taken completely by surprise, the man toppled from his horse with the ash pole through his throat.

With a roar, Falcon spurred his horse into the midst of his disconcerted foes. He tore his ax from its place and brought it down on a helmet with an audible crunch. Wulf sprang from his saddle and dashed to his master's left side. From this position, he repelled any of the footmen who tried to attack Falcon from his left rear, always a horseman's most vulnerable spot against foot attack.

The bandits were disconcerted for a moment at the fury of the attack, but they quickly regained the initiative and encircled the two men, the horsemen keeping them at lancepoint while the footmen rushed in for the kill like wolves.

"Break out, Draco!" Wulf shouted. "We can't beat them like this!"

"Mount behind me!" Falcon ordered. He knew that it was useless. The instant Wulf turned his back, he'd get an ax in it and even his excellent mail wouldn't save him.

Then there was a thunder of hooves and three horsemen were breaking through the circle of bandits, hewing right and left with their long swords. Falcon shouted with joyous rage at this unexpected aid, and then he was spurring back among the outlaws, his long, curved sword now out, flickering in bewildering arcs and dealing death or wounds at every cut. Within seconds, the remnants of the bandits were fleeing into the woods, where the trees grew too thick for mounted pursuit. Falcon chased them as far as the edge of the wood, then turned back to thank his rescuers.

Wulf ran up to him, holding out a piece of cloth cut from one of the bandits' tunics. As Falcon cleaned his blade, Wulf said in a low voice: "Look who we've fallen in with, my lord."

Falcon cantered over to the three knights. All wore excellent armor and face-covering helmets, which they were removing. All were dressed in identical white surcoats over their armor. The surcoats bore a red cross. Their shields were likewise white with red crosses. "Templars, by God!" Falcon whispered. He had reason to distrust the Knights of the Temple. He had seen the last of the old order cut down defending the Beauséant, famed standard of the Templars, at the disastrous battle of Hattin. The order had been rebuilt by Gerard de Ridemont, grand master of the Templars, and Falcon knew them to be something far more sinister than the crusading order they had been for so long. Still, these men had saved his life, and he had to put the best face on it. He cantered over to them.

"I am Sir Draco Falcon, and I thank you for your aid, good sirs."

One of the men threw back his coif to reveal sandy hair and blue eyes. He was very young, no more than about twenty-two. "I am Claude de Coucy," he said. "My brothers and I were on our way to the Temple outside Paris when some local people told us of these bandits and we rode looking for them. We are pleased to have found you in time to be of assistance." In spite of his distrust, Falcon found himself liking the young knight. The other two were older men who spoke little except curtly to acknowledge Falcon's thanks.

Gudrun and the other travelers came up, loud in their praise of Falcon and the Templars. "It was like some old hero tale," Gudrun exclaimed, "first Sir Draco taking on all those men by himself, then these gentlemen appearing just when all seemed lost." Wulf looked annoyed when his own part in the affray was slighted, but life had accustomed him to the insensitivity of his betters. "Will you ride with us to Paris?"

"We should be honored, lady," Sir Claude said, taking her hand and kissing it. The warrior-monks were supposed to be bound by a vow of chastity, but this one hadn't forgotten his courtly manners.

"With such men as you four riding with us," Gudrun said, "we need fear nothing." Falcon wanted nothing to do with Templars, but now there was nothing he could do about it. His jaw set in a grim line, he rode beside the white-robed men down the road to Paris.

TWO

FALCON SAT on the pile of his bedding under the shelter of his tent. It was not the big tent he slept in when campaigning. Instead, this tent was barely large enough for two men to stretch out in, and scarcely had headroom for a man as tall as Falcon to sit upright. Just now, Wulf lay outside the tent, preferring the clear night to the stuffy confines of the canvas.

Falcon was polishing his helmet, which was, like most of his gear, Saracen-made. Its design was rather old-fashioned; a tall cone with its peak canted slightly forward. A thick bar called a nasal protected the nose. Most such helmets were built up of several pieces of iron riveted to a frame, but Falcon's was crafted from a single piece of steel, its sides fluted and the whole so exquisitely tempered that had it not been heavily padded inside, it would have rung like a bell when struck.

Satisfied with the helmet's polish, he laid it aside and

pulled his mailshirt across his knees, going over every inch of it in search of rust. It looked much like a European hauberk, but where the Western armor was made of coarse hammered iron rings, Falcon's was constructed with fine drawn-steel wire. The individual rings were much smaller than on a European hauberk, and each ring passed through four others and then closed and fastened with a minute rivet. Over the chest, shoulders, and belly, the rings were of thicker wire, strong and more densely linked. The back, the wrist-length sleeves, and the skirts that hung to the knees were of thinner wire to conserve weight. The hauberk weighed perhaps one-third what a Western coat of similar proportions would have.

He stowed the hauberk in its oiled bag and took up the sword. This he always saved for last. He drew the curved blade from its sheath as sensuously as if he were caressing a lover. The curvature was slight, the blade wide and somewhat broader at the tip than at the hilt. It was of true Damascus make. In the Syrian hills, a small clan of smiths practiced the ancient art of forging bars of many qualities of steel into blades of incredible strength and keenness. When the final polishing was done, the blades had the appearance of watered silk, with rills and dapples of silver and gray covering the surface, the result of the many different steels that went into their construction. So complicated was the forging and tempering process that most Damascus blades were daggers or short swords. Few smiths attempted blades more than two feet in length. Falcon's sword was more than three feet long, its grip and pommel adding another foot to its length. In the East, it was a fabled weapon. Long ago, it had been named Three Moons, for the three crescents of blade, hilt, and pommel. When the sword was given to Falcon, he had renamed it Nemesis, for the ancient Grecian goddess of vengeance.

Satisfied that his weapons and armor were in perfect condition, Falcon took a pull at the skin of good red wine that hung from the tent's centerpole. The last rays of the sun faded and the bustle of the roadside camp quieted. The fires were small, for penalties were severe against those who cut wood in a baron's forest. Only fallen wood was lawful to gather, and the local peasants got most of that.

There were sounds from outside, and Wulf poked his shaggy head into the tent. "The friar's here and wants to talk to you," Wulf said.

"Tell him I've no need to confess," Falcon grumbled. The last thing he wanted was to talk with some meddling churchman.

"I've no doubt you stand in greater need of absolution than most men, Sir Draco." It was the voice of Fra Benedetto. "However, the condition of your soul is not my concern just now. It is a matter of business I wish to discuss, and it is rather urgent."

"Oh, very well," Falcon said, with poor grace. "Come in."

The friar made his way into the cramped tent. It was as well that he was a small man. Falcon held out the wineskin hospitably, and the friar took it. Instead of drinking from the spout, he produced a fine silver cup from inside his habit and poured it full. He raised the cup in salute and drank.

"Splendid wine," the friar pronounced.

"Your business?" Falcon asked. Offering the wine had exhausted his store of hospitality for this man.

"Sir Draco," Benedetto said, "how well are you acquainted with the situation of the empire?"

"Scarcely at all," Falcon said. What was this man driving at? "I know the old emperor died a few years ago and the throne's been vacant since. It's no business of mine. I'm just a free captain. All my dealings are with petty barons and such, so the doings of kings and emperors don't concern me."

"They concern some of us," the friar said. "The Lady Gudrun, for instance."

"Lady Gudrun? How so?"

"Did you really think," Benedetto said testily, "that that German cow was going to Paris for a social visit? She is an agent, Sir Draco; an agent for Otto of Brunswick, who hopes to be crowned emperor!"

"Then she has a difficult job ahead of her," Falcon said. "Otto was Richard's ally."

"But Richard is dead and now Philip Augustus is the most powerful king west of the Rhine. New lines must be drawn, because the King of England is a weakling. And who better to send than this Teutonic slut? Philip is a king of notoriously weak moral character."

Falcon smiled to hear this from a man like Fra Benedetto. "And you?" Falcon asked. "Who do you support?"

"Why I—that is to say, the Holy Father, of course, supports the Hohenstaufen claimant, Philip of Swabia."

"Hmm," Falcon mused, "another Philip. And the Holy Father planted you on Lady Gudrun to keep an eye on her and to press the Hohenstaufen suit at King Philip's court?"

"You make it sound as if I were spying," Benedetto said. "In truth, it was the Norse giantess who was spying at the papal court, under the guise of a holy pilgrim. I have been commissioned by the Holy Father to see that she does not misrepresent to King Philip the claims of Brunswick, and to counter her lies with a true account of the advantages to be gained by supporting Philip of Swabia."

"Those advantages being?" Falcon was becoming interested in spite of himself. He planned to become a great lord someday, so it was as well to start taking an interest in the complicated dynastic politics of Europe.

"Well," Benedetto said, "for one thing, the Holy Father might be persuaded to lift King Philip's ban of excommunication."

"Is Philip excommunicate these days?" Falcon asked.

"Didn't you know? Yes, ever since he put away his lawful wife, Ingeborg of Denmark, and married Agnes of Meran. France is under interdict."

By "France," of course, Benedetto referred only to the small territory Philip held by his own right. The other great counties held by the powerful nobles did not necessarily come under the papal ban. Under interdiction, no holy services could be held, and all who died were unshriven and could not be buried in hallowed ground. It was the Pope's most powerful weapon and had brought more than one king to his knees. Once, a Holy Roman Emperor had stood barefoot in the snow outside a papal castle, begging to have the interdiction lifted from his domains.

"I see," Falcon said. "But what have I to do with all this?"

"Sir Draco," Fra Benedetto said urgently, "I fear that I stand in need of protection. I have reason to believe that that Rhineland ogress suspects me of desiring to thwart her plans. She will stop at nothing to advance the claims of the false and ungodly Otto of Brunswick, not even murder.

"Sir Draco, as a knight, you are pledged to support the church and her minions—to wit, priests, nuns, monks, and friars."

"That is so," Falcon said. "However, I am also pledged to support and protect ladies of gentle birth. Lady Gudrun is one such."

"Well, yes, but—I am willing, of course, to reward you for your troubles."

"To what extent?" Falcon asked. Business at last.

"Twenty gold florins?" Benedetto queried.

Falcon clapped the friar on the shoulder, nearly toppling him over. "Friar, I'll deliver you safe and sound to King Philip's doorstep, in one piece and with no parts missing that are there now."

"I am most relieved, Sir Draco." He thought a moment, then a look of doubt crossed his face. "But what if the barbarian witch tries poison?"

Surely this shivering friar didn't expect him to be his food taster for the duration of the journey? A sudden inspiration came to Falcon. He reached into a bag and drew forth an amulet. It was disc-shaped and was pierced with a hole in its center, through which a leather thong was threaded. It was made of brass and was marked with Arabic lettering. He handed it to the friar.

"Fra Benedetto," Falcon said earnestly, "this was given to me by a very holy hermit in Palestine, in gratitude for my saving his life. If you dip it into your winecup before drinking, or wave it over your food while reciting a paternoster, it will preserve you from poison. You may keep it until we reach Paris, but you must return it to me then."

"Why, thank you, Sir Draco." Fra Benedetto gazed at the thing in admiration. "Would you consider selling this?"

"No," Falcon said with great conviction. "Something as precious as this I must keep in my family." Another thought came to him. "But I must warn you: It has power only so long as the user does not try to use poison on someone else. I know, of course, that you would never do such a thing, but I must tell you of the amulet's limitations."

"Oh," said Benedetto, sounding slightly disappointed, "well, it is good to know that I shall be safe from the wiles of that Gothic hoyden."

"Half now," Falcon said, holding out a callused palm.

"What? Of, of course." The friar took out a purse and counted out ten golden florins. He put the amulet in the purse, returned purse and cup to the interior of his garments, and rose to leave. "Rest tonight assured of a safe journey," Falcon said.

When the friar had left, Falcon sat testing each of the coins for soundness. All were good. That was one good thing about dealing with Italians. North of the Alps, there was always a shortage of coin, and even kings had to accept their taxes in produce, livestock, and bolts of cloth. Italians always seemed to have ready cash, and much of it wasn't counterfeit.

Falcon chuckled. He'd deliver Fra Benedetto safe and sound, all right. He'd undertaken the protection of this group, so he would have done that anyway. Now he was ten florins ahead, with the prospect of ten more. As for the chance of Lady Gudrun's trying to poison the friar, Falcon was certain that Benedetto's timidity and suspicion were getting the better of him. Gudrun looked like the kind of woman who if she took it into her head to kill a man would use an ax.

As for the amulet, Falcon did hope to get that back. He had won it at dice from a Greek sailor in Constantinople. It was a token, good for one sex act of his choice at a famous bordello in Alexandria.

"What business takes you to Paris, Sir Draco?"

22

asked the young Templar, Claude de Coucy. He seemed honest and without guile, but Falcon knew too much about the Templars to let his guard down.

"A matter of employment for myself and my men," Falcon answered.

"Employment? You mean you go to swear homage to a liege?"

"No. My men and I serve for money—for a specified period of time, or until the accomplishment of a campaign, or until the money runs out. My men have sworn fealty to me, and I find employment for them."

"I've heard that that's how it's done in the Holy Land," Claude said. "I didn't know that anyone was soldiering that way here. Have you been successful?"

"We've not lacked for work," Falcon said. "There's always a little war going on someplace, and lords are always in need of men. Their knights give their forty days' service each year and then they decamp and go home, even if it's in the middle of a siege or they face battle the next day. Most are grateful to find men who will soldier on at any time and in any weather."

"As long as the pay holds out," Sir Claude amended.

"That's understood. No pay, no service."

"It sounds like a good life," the Templar said wistfully.

"How did you come to join the Temple?" Falcon asked. "You sound like a man who'd rather be out free-lancing."

"It's in the family," Claude said. "When my mother died, my father turned the castle and lands over to my older brother and went on pilgrimage to the Holy Land. There he joined the Templars. He died gloriously at Hattin."

"They were good soldiers who died at Hattin," Falcon said noncommittally. "I was there."

23

"You were at Hattin!" The young knight's face lit with excitement. "Were you near the Templars?"

"I was with Raymond of Tripoli that day," Falcon said. "That's why I'm alive. I saw the last of the Templars fall."

One of the older Templars rode up, forcing his mount between Falcon and Claude. "Raymond of Tripoli?" the Templar said. "He was no friend of the Temple."

Falcon glared at the knight. "Raymond and the grand master were on bad terms. Their enmity predated Gerard's joining the Temple."

A third Templar rode up on Claude's other side. The first stared at Falcon without favor. He had a grizzled beard that protruded from his mail coif in tufts. "Our brother goes to the Paris Temple to take his final vows," he said. "I think it would be best for him to spend the rest of the journey in prayer and meditation." The two older Templars rode off with Claude between them. Falcon shrugged. It was none of his business.

Falcon sat in his tent, going through his nightly ritual of checking his equipment. It was getting dark, and he had had Wulf fetch him a candle, which gave him just enough light for the task at hand. In addition, he had ordered two cups set out on a low stool he had borrowed from a harper in the band.

As soon as complete darkness had fallen, the visitor he was expecting arrived. He was pouring wine into both cups when Wulf's head appeared in the doorway. "It's the lady this time. Shall I let her in?" Falcon nodded.

Lady Gudrun squeezed herself into the tent, which she filled far more substantially than Fra Benedetto had. Falcon had no objection to this.

"Ah, Sir Draco," she said, "how good of you to receive me." He handed her a cup, and she drained it instantly. "Thank you, you are most gracious." She held the cup out and Falcon refilled it.

"Sir Draco," she began, "while of course I esteem the company of so chivalrous a knight as yourself, you must understand that I come here unaccompanied, trusting in your sense of honor, because I require your protection."

"Ah, I see," Falcon said.

"I suppose, Sir Draco, that you think Fra Benedetto is a mere papal emissary, sent to exchange pleasantries with King Philip's diplomats?"

"I confess that was my impression," Falcon said.

"Be assured, Sir Draco, he is nothing of the sort!" For emphasis she took a deep breath, nearly bursting the seams of her gown. Tonight she was wearing white samite that appeared to be somewhat thinner than paint. Falcon refilled her cup, which had once again gone dry.

"Fra Benedetto," Gudrun continued, "is an agent sent by the Pope to trick King Philip into an alliance with Philip of Swabia, the spurious upstart who plans to seize the empire for himself!"

"Say you so?" Falcon commented. "Do go on." There followed a recitation much like the one he had heard the night before from Benedetto, save with a slight change of bias. During her heartfelt tirade in support of Otto of Brunswick, Gudrun loosened her coif and wimple and pulled them off, loosing a cascade of wavy ash-white hair which fell to her ample hips. Her face grew flushed with enthusiasm and wine during her recitation.

"My lady," Falcon said when she paused to draw breath, "I applaud your championship of the undoubted virtues of Otto of Brunswick. How may a humble, landless knight like myself be of service to you?" He picked up the wineskin. It was flat as a beggar's purse. He stuck his head outside. "Wulf, fetch another skin of this wine." Grumbling, the Saxon stumbled off in search of more wine.

"Sir Draco," Gudrun said, "I fear that I am in need of protection."

"In truth?" Falcon said, calling up his best imitation of amazement.

"Most assuredly. I would not be at all surprised if those bandits you so efficiently disposed of were hired by the friar for the sole purpose of doing away with me!"

Falcon forbore to remark on the extreme unlikelihood of this. Wulf thrust a full wineskin into the tent. Falcon seized it and refilled Gudrun's cup.

She disposed of the wine at a gulp and held the cup for refilling. "Ah, thank you. Sir Draco, you are a chivalrous knight and I must beg your protection."

"It shall be my honor, my lady. Of course, my man and I are but poor men, and we are accustomed to being . . ." He let the sentence taper off, lest he sully his relationship with this aristocratic lady by hinting at the ignoble subject of money.

"Of course, I know that you will require a token recompense. Fifteen gold florins?"

"Twenty is the customary sum," Falcon murmured.

"Even so. Twenty." She leaned back against the wall of the cramped tent, her business done. A new light came into her eye, and Falcon grew apprehensive.

"Sir Draco, I hope you will not think me bold if I observe that you are a fine figure of a man."

"My lady is too kind," Falcon said, eying the entrance as if looking for escape. Gudrun grasped his

26

hand and held it to her prodigious breast. He could feel the rock-hardness of the tiny nipple. Amazingly, he could also feel the powerful beating of her heart through the considerable bulk of her breast.

"Sir Draco," she said huskily, "when I first saw you, I knew that you would be my paladin. I am a poor widow, all alone in the world. I need the attentions of a knight of manhood and breeding. Let us not stand upon the rigors of formality." With no further ado, she began ripping loose the laces of her bodice. The tent! Falcon thought. She'll destroy it, the randy Amazon! Then another thought came. All those people out there! He just knew that this woman would be noisy.

In the meantime, Gudrun had pulled her gown down, so that her breasts sprang free of their confinement. Like most fashionable ladies, Gudrun dispensed with undergarments in warm weather. Her waist was surprisingly small, her belly gracefully mounded. She shoved the samite past her broad hips and powerful thighs. God, what a woman! he thought.

She seized Falcon and kissed him deeply, her tongue thrusting past his teeth. With a free hand, she began unlacing his hose. She reached inside and grasped her prey. "Ah, Sir Draco, you are a man indeed!" She undressed him so quickly that he was not quite sure how it happened.

"My lady," Falcon said, "the candle, if you please. This tent is lit up like a lantern from outside." Gudrun blew out the light. She pushed him back on his pallet, then straddled him, her knees planted at either side of his waist. Reaching down to guide him, she lowered herself until she was fully impaled and gave vent to a sigh that could have been heard for a mile in any direction. She began to rock her hips back and forth, and as she did she reached for the wineskin.

Falcon watched in amazement as at least a quart disappeared down her throat. She held the skin to his mouth and squeezed it. Falcon swallowed thirstily. He knew that he was going to need it.

Around midnight, Falcon found himself atop Gudrun, her legs around his waist in a spine-cracking grip. He was thrusting away for all he was worth, dripping sweat like a summer rainstorm. "Ah, Sir Draco," Gudrun said gustily, "you do know how to couch your lance!" She reached for a full wineskin and took a long pull. Four empty ones were wadded into a corner of the tent. Wulf had been throwing them in as they were called for. She dropped the skin and ran her hands over his hard-knotted muscles, then gave him a hard slap on the buttocks. "Ride, my chevalier. You have a hard gallop to accomplish before this night is over!"

Falcon mounted his horse, wincing as his lower parts came in contact with the saddle. He had wiped Wulf's grin away with a sound kick in the rear, but all the travelers had faces similarly graced. He flushed with chagrin when one of the jongleurs began singing an extempore song about "the Norman stallion and the German mare." There was nothing to be done about it.

Wulf had had to peel the tent off him when the sun rose. All the pegs were torn up and the ropes in a tangle. Falcon's head throbbed and rang like a cathedral bell. Worst of all, at some time during their tempestuous lovemaking, Gudrun had worked him down to ten florins.

Fra Bendetto rode up to him. "Sir Draco," he said scornfully, "is this how you protect me? By consorting with that Alemannic harlot?"

Falcon favored the friar with a look that would have turned a rhinoceros to stone. "I assure you, friar, that for the entirety of last night, you were in no danger from Lady Gudrun."

THREE

THE FIELDS around Paris were lively. The harvest was in, and it had been a good one. Now the stubble was being burned off and the peasants were driving the pigs into the forests to fatten upon the acorns on the woodland floor in preparation for fall slaughter. There would be good eating until late winter, when the season of Lent would make a virtue of necessity.

Falcon was still getting over the soreness and bruises of his tumble with Gudrun. He had emerged from sizable battles with fewer infirmities. The woman's appetites were in proportion to her size and endowments. Even his jaw felt as if he'd taken a mace clout across it.

Their first sight of Paris was of the towering spires of Notre Dame, visible long before they saw the city walls. The road was thronged now. There were peasants going to the city to sell produce, artisans headed for the many royal building projects, students for the schools, entertainers for the fairs, and a large number of knights. Falcon found out by questioning that the knights were gathering for a huge royal tourney to be held in a few days. The event had been proclaimed for months in France and abroad, but this was the first he'd heard of it. He had no intention of taking part. Tourneys could be profitable, for a loser's arms and mount went to the winner, to be ransomed back at a fixed sum, but Falcon found the possible profits to be in no way commensurate with the risks involved. A knight risked death or injury, and so did his horse. In the scramble of the melee, there was as much luck as skill involved in coming out victorious and in one piece.

The Templars parted company with the travelers just before reaching the city. The Paris Temple was a short distance outside the city walls. Falcon was not sorry to see the last of them.

At the gates, they were waved through; the guards had neither the time nor the manpower to check every entrant. The gates would be shut at sundown, and in the meantime any who wanted could pass. The party split up as soon as they were within the city. Gudrun and Fra Benedetto bade Falcon farewell as they went toward the palace, and Falcon and Wulf went in search of an inn. There was none to be found that had room. Paris was an overcrowded city at the best of times, and with the royal court in residence and the tourney imminent, the throng was almost impenetrable. Had they not been mounted and able to force a way with the weight of their horses, it would have taken them hours to traverse the length of a single street.

Wulf mounted wearily after being rejected for a tenth time. "We might as well be Joseph and Mary on the night of Nativity," he grumbled. "That innkeeper said we should try a place called the Latin Quarter. What's that?"

"Near the cathedral," Falcon said. "It's where most of the students live. We may as well try, I suppose." By asking directions, they found a bridge to cross the Seine onto the island which had once lodged the whole city. It was, if anything, even more crowded than the greater city, with narrow, winding streets and gabled buildings with overhanging upper floors that almost met overhead. From time to time they heard the cry of *"Gardez l'eau!"* and spurred their horses to safety as the contents of a chamber pot were flung from an upper window into the street below. There was much cursing as those who failed to move quickly enough were showered.

The smells of the city were indescribable. There were cooking smells, animal smells, human smells, the stench of the filthy streets, the smoke of fires. Over all hung the reek of the city's tanneries and slaughter-houses, where the blood of slaughtered beasts was customarily simply poured into the streets, to make its way to the river as best it might. To Falcon and Wulf, used to the clean air of the countryside, the stench was overpowering.

"God!" Wulf swore, "At least in London the laws make them keep the city clean. Even Rome is better than this."

At length they found a tavern called the Two Swords. The owner gave them a corner of an upstairs room where they could stow their goods and sleep on the straw. He promised that there would be no more than ten others to share the room. It was inconvenient, but they had endured worse.

After leaving their bags they went to the stables in back to see to their mounts. Falcon's was a destrier: a dangerous beast that could not be handled by an ordinary hostler. Since Wulf ordinarily fought on foot, his horse was a courser: a fleet-footed hunting mount. By law, Wulf's rank allowed him to ride only a common hackney, but the animal belonged to Falcon. In any case, the two seldom paid attention to the all-embracing sumptuary laws, which were spottily enforced at best.

Assured that the stalls were clean and the beasts well cared for, they went into the common room. It was beginning to fill, for the next day was a holiday and the students were pouring in, their day's classes over. There was a babble of many tongues, for students formed an international community, united by the Latin which was the language of all schools and which gave the student quarter its title. The room was low-ceilinged, with smoke-stained beams from which hung strings of onions and garlic and sausages. At the rear, a huge fire blazed, and carcasses turned before it on spits turned by a pair of urchins.

Falcon and Wulf found places at a table occupied only by a burly knight with a big black mustache. The knight introduced himself as Hugh de Chartres and hospitably made room for them. They ordered food and ale, which were quickly brought: a basket of loaves and tubs of butter, joints of pork, and a bowl of boiled leeks and turnips. The table already bore baskets of fruit and cheeses. They set to with the relish of hungry soldiers, for breakfast had been many hours since.

"I love the fall," Wulf sighed. "Eating's always best in the fall."

"Are you here for the tourney?" Hugh asked Draco.

"No. I'm here to see a vassal of the Viscount of Limoges," Falcon answered. "He has some employment for me and my men. I don't know what it is, but they'll skin me if I get myself wounded in a tourney before I can transact our business."

Hugh reached into his purse and withdrew a folded parchment. It crackled as he unfolded and smoothed it. He held it close to his eyes. "This was given to me by a royal herald at Chartres. It's supposed to give the particulars of the tourney, but I'm damned if I can make sense of it." Falcon was not surprised. The man was holding it upside down. "I'm damned if I'll ask one of these damned uppity students to read it for me, though. Do you see a churchman about?" The knight sniffed at the parchment as if its matter could be transmitted by scent.

Falcon took the parchment and righted it. It was old and dingy, washed and scraped for reuse so many times that it was nearly transparent. It was written in court French by the hand of an indifferent clerk.

"All knights and squires of gentle birth," Falcon intoned, "are hereby invited to participate in a grand royal tourney to be held at Paris after the ides of October, to commence upon the first day of clear weather." Hugh gaped at him. Few knights were literate. Many kings were not. "There will be jousting by challenge upon the first day. The champion of the joust shall name the Queen of Love and Beauty. The last day of the tourney shall end with a grand melee. Afterward, all participants are invited to a royal banquet at the palace. Long live Philipus Augustus, Rex."

Falcon gave back the parchment and picked up a joint of pork, which he tore into with his strong white teeth. Hugh did not disturb him while he ate, but the knight was clearly bursting with curiosity. At length, Falcon leaned back, replete. The recitation had also attracted the attention of some students, who were likewise astonished at the spectacle of a literate knight.

"Forgive me, Sir Draco, but were you trained for the priesthood in your youth?" Hugh asked.

"No," Falcon said noncommittally.

"Sir Draco Falcon?" said a student at a nearby table. "Isn't there a song making the rounds about such a one?"

"Not that I'd heard," Falcon said.

"Of course there is," said a student, a stringy youth with a straggly yellow beard. "Where's that jongleur?" He looked about until he spotted a man with a harp sitting by the hearth. "Hey, Savinien, give us the song about Falcon and the siege of Pierre Noir!"

The tattered entertainer stepped into the center of the room and strummed his harp. All fell silent until he was satisfied with the instrument's tuning. Then he launched into his song of the wondrous doings at Pierre Noir: how Sir Draco Falcon, the stainless knight-errant, had come to rescue the wondrous beauty Marie de Cleves; how he had fought his way through the legions of the evil orgre Lord Thibaut; how he had single-handedly slain a hundred Saracens commanded by the renegade Crusader Gunther Valdemar; how he had slain Valdemar in a trial by combat that had lasted three days and three nights; how he had finally besieged the mighty castle of Pierre Noir and slain the twenty-foot ogre Thibaut with his enchanted sword, freeing the beauteous Marie from her magical chains, whereupon she had shown herself to be a fairy princess and rewarded him with a ring which would grant him three wishes.

At the end of his song, the jongleur bowed to the general applause and Falcon tossed him a silver coin.

"I'm afraid it wasn't quite like that," Falcon confided to Hugh. "There were only two Saracens. They tried to kill me in my tent one night, but I killed them first. Marie's a pretty lass, but no fairy princess. Thibaut was a coward—a hunchback with a withered leg. One of my men smothered him in a pile of dogshit. The trial by combat with Valdemar happened, though. Now *that* was a fight, though it lasted less than half an hour."

"I wish I'd seen it," Hugh said. "Damned jongleurs. They do exaggerate, don't they?"

The stringy blond student came to their table and asked permission to sit, which was granted. "Are you really the Draco Falcon of the song?" he asked.

"I am Falcon, and I conducted the siege of Pierre Noir, but the Draco of the song exists only in the minds of jongleurs."

The student laughed. "I suspected as much, but where would we be without the thoughts of philosophers and the wonders of poets? I am Mika son of Vaino, from Finland, though I was raised in Uppsala, in Sweden. I study theology and philosophy at the cathedral school." The youth wore a shabby student's robe, and like the other students he was belted with a short sword and dagger. The riots between students and townsmen were notorious, and a student took his life in his hands by appearing outside the Quarter alone and unarmed.

A contest began among the students, each trying to recite a line of poetry which began with the word which had ended the line given by the student before. While this was going on, Falcon questioned Mika about his travels. Falcon had never met a Finn, and was fascinated by stories of doings in the remote north. Wulf was growing restive, having already downed too much ale, his ear abraded by the mincing French and Provençal of the bandied poems. He could stand no more. He lurched to his feet and pounded on the table.

"You call that poetry?" Wulf shouted. "I'll give

36

you a poem! Listen to some real verses." In a rich
voice he began to chant:

"Mæg ic be mē sylfum   sōdgied wrecan
sībpas secgan   hu ic geswincdagum
earfordhwīle   oft prō wade,
bitre breostceare   gebiden hæbbe
gecunnad in ceole   cearselda fela
atol ybpa gewealc.   pær mec oft bigeat . . ."

Falcon sighed. In his cups, Wulf had a tendency to
roar out his native Saxon verse. It often led to trouble.
"Cease that Gothic braying, you barbarian lout!"
shouted a student. Wulf crossed the room and fed the
student a buffet on the jaw that stretched him sense-
less on the straw-covered floor. Wulf resumed his
seat. "Milk-fed sodomites!" Wulf fumed. "They have
no appreciation of good verse. I knew *Beowulf* by
heart before I killed my first tax collector. I was only
twelve then." Falcon knew this to be untrue, but saw
no point in bringing the fact up.
    A heated argument now sprang up over some
newly translated works of Aristotle. Some held that
the translation, which was from Arabic, was accurate,
others that it was full of flaws. Swords were being
drawn when the tavernkeeper appeared with a short
club. He quieted the discussion with a few solid raps
on some tonsured pates.
    "Damned school authorities," Mika said. He was a
little the worse for all the wine he had put away.
"Bishop says we shouldn't include Aristotle in the
curriculum. Says he's a heathen and has nothing to
teach Christians. What's he know? Aristotle was the
greatest man who ever lived, by Christ! I exclude
Christ himself, of course," he added hastily. "He
wasn't exactly a man, anyway."

"Damn all heathens, anyway," mumbled Hugh, dipping his mustache into his ale.

"Ever heard of Aristotle, Sir Draco?" asked Mika.

"I've read some of his works," Falcon admitted, the ale he had shipped, some two or three quarts, loosening his usually reticent tongue. "A few of the *Dialogues*, *On Politics*, *On Monarchy*, *The Categories*, *The Topics*, things like that. What else? Oh, let's see, there was *Prior* and *Posterior Analytics*, the *Organon*, the *Rhetoric*, *Poetics* and *Ethics*, there was something called *Physics*, though I never understood the tenth part of that. What else? There was something called *De Anima*, but I only got partway through that."

Mika's thin-bearded jaw had dropped as far as his chest. He was shocked almost sober. Most of the works Falcon had named had never been translated into Latin. Except for a few minor works in ancient Latin translation, the whole of Aristotle had been lost during the Dark Ages. The works had been preserved in Greek, and Arabic scholars had translated them into their own tongue, from which doctors who had accompanied the Crusades were laboriously translating them into Latin. So far, only a few works were trickling into the European schools.

"By God!" Mika swore. "Who was your teacher?" Some of the other students had heard Falcon's recitation, and were crowding themselves onto the benches around the table.

"The learned Dr. Abraham of Toledo," Falcon said.

"You're talking too much, my lord," Wulf said.

"Abraham of Toledo!" marveled a student. "The friend of Averröes? You've studied under Abraham?"

"Damn all Jews, anyway," mumbled Hugh, downing a quart of ale. "All Saracens, too, by God!" Quietly, the knight slid from the bench onto the straw beneath the table, where he began to snore peacefully.

His place was quickly taken by a student. They all wanted to hear about these new works of Aristotle.

"Then you must know Arabic!" said one.

"I was a prisoner for many years in Palestine," Falcon answered. "I served in a household where Abraham was a guest." His face took on a faraway look as he remembered Miriam, Abraham's daughter. She had taught him far more than Abraham had. "Enough!" he said suddenly. He tried to get to his feet, but the students bore him down. They refilled his mug and thrust it into his hands.

"*The Analytics*!" shouted one. "Do you know *The Analytics*, Sir Draco? We've only heard the name!"

"Yes, I studied that," he said morosely. He'd talked himself into this. Damn his loose tongue! For the next two hours, he lectured on the subjects he half remembered from his years as the servant of Suleiman the Wise, when Abraham had been his friend and teacher. Imperfect as his memory was, the students drank in his words as if they had been fine wine.

He had taken up the studies only because Suleiman had insisted upon it. He had only been interested in learning the arts of Suleiman's incredible swordsmanship, but the old man had insisted that he would only teach a whole man, not a mere killer. He was amazed at how much he could recall. Raised in an illiterate society, where the main entertainment was the recitation of interminable heroic poems and long genealogies, his mind was trained to the retention of huge volumes of verse, so the thoughts of Aristotle poured from his lips, along with Abraham's commentaries, just as he'd heard them. It was an irony that these students could comprehend the words far better than he, who had heard them from the lips of a master.

The door slammed open and a band of youths crowded themselves into the common room. They were tough, hard-bitten young men, their brown-stained hands proclaiming them to be apprentices from the local tanneries. They shouted for ale and truculently glared about them, eying the students with disfavor.

"Trouble just came in," muttered a student. "We'll not escape a bout with those bullyboys before the night's out." Surreptitiously, the students were loosening the cords that bound their swords in their sheaths. Falcon eyed the apprentices. All wore daggers, and most had wooden truncheons hanging from their belts. Falcon's sword was with his gear. Just as well, he thought. He had no taste for a killing in a casual brawl, especially in a strange town, where the courts would give short shrift to a landless knight opposing townsmen.

The students urged Falcon to resume his impromptu lecture upon Aristotle, but his heart was not in it. His belly was heavy with dinner, and his head light from too much ale, and now he faced a brawl in which he had no interest when all he wanted was a good night's sleep.

Two of the apprentices came swaggering over to the table where Falcon sat. They wore the fixed sneer of street toughs everywhere. "Studying late, are you?" said one. "That's a strange-looking teacher you have there." They bristled with the resentment of the lower classes for their highly educated betters. As children of the working classes, they saw all students as useless, privileged parasites. The behavior of the students, often overbearing, condescending, and obnoxious, frequently made the attitude seem well justified.

"Leave us," Mika said. "We are discussing things beyond your lumpish minds." Falcon stifled a groan. Now they were in for it.

"Lumpish is it, you tonsured jackdaw?" raged an apprentice. "I'll give you a lump!" He cracked Mika across the brow with his truncheon, sending the Finnish youth sprawling. Falcon lurched to his feet, seized the youth by his stained doublet, and lifted him clear of the floor with one hand. He shook the man two or three times and threw him back to topple into the crowd of his friends, sending several to tumble into the straw. Another lunged at Falcon, but Wulf kicked his feet out from under him, and as he fell a student kicked him soundly in the head.

The sound of the fight brought Hugh de Chartres up off the floor, grinning and laying about him indiscriminately. He flattened a student and turned to Falcon. "Who are we fighting?" he asked.

"Those brown-handed villeins over there," Falcon said. "The students are on our side."

"Oh," Hugh said. He looked down at the student he had struck, who was rubbing a rapidly swelling jaw. "Sorry," said the knight.

The tanners waded in as a group, swinging their clubs. Swords were out now, and the students were slashing away merrily, whooping and shouting. Brawls with townsmen were a favorite pastime, a welcome relief from the tedium of studies. Fortunately for all concerned, the swords weren't very sharp, being more like iron clubs than battle weapons. Falcon picked up the bench he'd been sitting on, spilling a drunken student to the straw. He lifted the heavy wooden bench overhead and cast it into the mass of the tanners, dropping several.

Three of the tanners bore down upon Falcon. He kicked one in the stomach and fed another an elbow, feeling teeth crack as the youth collapsed. He grasped the third by the shoulder and spun him around, then booted him in the buttocks. The tanner staggered across the room and crashed headfirst into the hearth, where a spitboy pulled him out of the fire amid a cloud of smoke, pungent with singing hair. The boy then went back to basting a goose.

Falcon saw Wulf go down under a crowd of tanners and waded with Hugh over to the knot of men. The two knights plucked men from the writhing pile, kneeing and elbowing and stomping them into submission. As they neared the bottom of the heap, they could hear a Saxon battle song, which had been composed for more heroic events. Falcon was careful never to strike with his fists. He knew that the human hand contained some of the most fragile, easily broken bones in the body, and he considered striking a skull, the most rugged of bones, to be the height of folly.

The two knights hauled Wulf to his feet amid a tangle of semi-inert forms. They were now in a comparatively tranquil area, but the fighting continued unabated all around. Here and there a small group of tanners kicked a fallen student, while at other spots a knot of students were rendering the same courtesy to a felled tanner.

Word of the riot had spread, and now butchers, shoemakers, and carpenters were pouring into the tavern, armed with the tools of their trades: cleavers, awls, and wooden mauls. Things were getting out of hand. Students were pouring in from the nearby dormitories, and from the sound of it the fighting had spread to the street outside. It was only a matter of time before the watch arrived.

Falcon saw a man stagger through the door, an arrow through his shoulder. It was getting serious indeed. "Time for us to get out of this." Falcon said. "Is there a back door to this place?"

Wulf picked up a fallen truncheon and smashed an attacking tanner across the face. The man reeled back, spitting blood and teeth. "You know this place as well as I do, my lord," the Saxon said.

Hugh grasped two tanners by the scruff of their necks and cracked their skulls together. He dropped the two and said: "Over there by the big ale tun there's a door. Let's go find a place where a man can get drunk in peace."

The three began to make their way to the back door, flattening an occasional attacker as they went. They thus made the mistake of all facing the same way at once. Two tanners lifted a heavy bench over their heads and lumbered up behind the three retiring warriors. The bench came down and Falcon was aware of a sudden, strangely beautiful flash of brilliant light. As he sank to the bloody straw, his last thoughts were of the sublime, utterly irrelevant words of that incomparable philosopher Aristotle.

FOUR

Wulf awoke with a splitting headache. He lay on a hard stone floor with a score of other men. Next to him was sitting Mika, the Finn. High, narrow windows admitted a dim light, and there was a single low door. The door had a small window, heavily barred.

"Where are we?" Wulf groaned.

"We're in jail," Mika said.

"Tell me more," Wulf demanded. He knew a jail when he saw one, having been in many.

"This is the student jail of the cathedral school," Mika elucidated.

"Where's my master?" Wulf asked, looking around in vain for Falcon.

"He and the other knight were taken to the Louvre," Mika answered.

"What's the Louvre?"

"It's an ancient tower in the city wall. It's used as a civil jail."

44

"Why was I brought here, then?" Wulf asked.

"It's your bald spot," Mika said, laughing. He winced at the pain his laughter caused to his injured jaw. "The watch thought you were tonsured and took you for a student."

Wulf rubbed the top of his head, which had several unfamiliar new lumps. Like many soldiers, he had a small bald area on his crown, caused by the constant rubbing of his helmet. The students shaved a small portion of their crowns, in token of their semi-ecclesiastical status.

Wulf was gripped by sudden stomach heaves. Mika pointed to a wooden bucket in a corner, and the Saxon made his way on hands and knees to it. He leaned over the bucket and retched violently. The bucket was redolent of its former users.

His stomach emptied, Wulf crawled back beside Mika. "Getting knocked on the head always makes me puke," he observed. "Next time I go to a student tavern I'll wear helmet and mail."

"That would be prudent," Mika said. "I often wear armor under my gown. See?" He opened his student gown to reveal the links of an old, rusty mailshirt. "Saved my life last night, for sure. A couple of butchers had me down and were hacking at me with their cleavers. My mail just dulled their blades."

"How many were killed?" Wulf asked.

"I don't know. I've seen as many as twenty dead after a good town-and-gown riot," Mika chuckled. "They'll think twice before they try to fight us students again." Wulf sincerely doubted this.

A student dragged himself over to where Wulf and Mika were sprawled. He had suffered a severe stab wound in the thigh, which was still oozing blood and clear fluid "Hey, Saxon," the student said, "your master was just getting into *The Analytics* when those tanners arrived. Did he, by any chance, ever discuss them with you? I'd like to hear the rest."

"Up your ass with Aristotle and all his boy-humping Greeks," Wulf groaned. He had been among some madmen in his time, but these were the worst.

"It's a good thing this is a holiday," Mika remarked philosophically. "Otherwise we'd be missing lectures."

"I can think of better places to spend a holiday," Wulf said.

"I seem to spend most of mine here," Mika said. "Odd, isn't it?"

Wulf didn't find it at all odd. The oddity was that these veteran brawlers found time for classes at all.

"Will we have a hearing?" Wulf asked.

"Pretty soon," Mika answered. "You'll probably be dismissed, because you aren't a student and the church court can't try you."

"That's one of the reasons the townsmen hate us so much," said the student with the wounded thigh. "The church claims us as her minions, so we're immune from civil law. We can be tried only in church courts."

"The townsmen are trying to change that, though," Mika said. "They say that because most of us go out into civil life to be lawyers and physicians and such, we should come under civil law. If that happens . . ." He let the words trail off in a tone of horror.

"Then," the other student said, "it'll be the rack for us. The scourge, the branding iron, the stocks, the public executioner, all the things those tanners are going through right now." The student chuckled at the thought of what the tanners must be enduring at that moment.

Wulf was supremely uninterested in the privileges of the students. What concerned him at the moment was how to get his master out of his predicament.

"Now, if we just had a charter from the king," Mika said, "that would solve everything. Until now, all has been ruled by custom. As they say, 'Twice makes a custom.' We think it's worked fine, but the city magistrates want to have things settled by law or royal decree."

"Piss on that," Wulf said. "We've got to get my master out of jail."

"That's very true," said the wounded student. "Otherwise, we'll never get to hear the rest of *The Analytics*."

Wulf groaned.

About midday, a priest appeared, accompanied by a burly monk who bore a scourge: a whip with a dozen or so thongs, studded with sheep's knucklebones.

"On your feet, you young Hittites," barked the priest. "It's the tribunal for you." The students lurched to their feet, moaning and hobbling, some having to be supported by friends. They filed from the jail, and Wulf followed them for lack of anything better to do. They went out into a courtyard where the sound of chanting could be heard. They were somewhere within the Notre Dame enclosure, but that was all Wulf could figure out.

They were led to a long chapter room, high-vaulted and lined with chairs in which sat severe-faced churchmen. The students stood in a huddled mass as a stern-looking man with an ascetic face rose to his feet. He wore a cowled black robe and he looked distinctly uncomfortable. Wulf guessed that he wore a hair shirt or barbed chains or some other flesh-mortifying device beneath the robe. Just what I need in a judge, he thought, someone who thinks suffering is good for the soul.

"Once again," intoned the ascetic, "you students have disgraced the cathedral school with your riots

47

and whorings and wantonings. You drink to befuddle-ment, and consort with loose women!" Wulf looked around and saw students trying to keep from grinning at pleasant memories. "Even worse!" the priest contin-ued. "You sing blasphemous songs, dance uproari-ously, play chess on the Sabbath, and eat meat on days of abstinence! You are sinners who shall burn in eter-nal hellfire unless you mend your ways!" He raised a fist in righteous indignation as the students hung their heads in prudent shame.

"However," the priest went on, in a calmer tone, "on this occasion, the offense has been a mere brawl, in which some two or three score townsmen and students were wounded in varying degrees of severity. You seem to have suffered in about the same degree as you inflicted injuries, so there is little to choose be-tween the plaintiffs of the case." He swept the little throng with a fanatical gaze. "However, the cause of this brawl stemmed from your indulgence in"— he glared about ferociously—"Aristotle!" He calmed himself with a visible effort. "If you must do battle, do it like Crusaders, in the name of our Lord Jesus Christ, not in that of some heathen sodomite!" The students winced to hear their hero so derided.

The priest extended a skinny finger toward Wulf. "I don't recognize you. Are you a new student, you young Edomite?"

"My name is Aethelwulf Ecgbehrtsson, your, ah, grace or whatever. I am a student of war, the servant of the great knight Sir Draco Falcon!" Wulf saw no point in being humble.

"A soldier!" said the priest disgustedly. "It was bad enough when you students consorted with nothing lower than whores. Stand aside, young man; this court has no business with you. As for the rest of you, you will suffer scourging. Prepare yourselves."

Sighing resignedly, the students lowered their hose, baring their pale buttocks. They formed a line and bent over, a few of them collapsing from the effort. The monk strode down the line, giving each a half-dozen lashes with his scourge, drawing blood by the third blow. There were loud moans, for many already bore stab wounds, slashes, and bruises in those parts. As the scourging ended, each straightened and pulled up his hose.

"That will be all," the priest said. "Classes in the morning at the usual time. Leave this place, young Philistines."

The students shuffled out, groaning and hissing from their pains. Wulf went with them.

"Is that all?" he asked Mika. "They just flog you like little boys and turn you loose?" He had expected a few exemplary hangings, at least.

"What else?" said the Finn, massaging his sore buttocks. "The school needs students as much as we need the school. After all, it's we who pay the professors, not the church. We fine them when they don't show up for lectures, and when attendance is too low. We provide the housing and entertainment. We throw the banquets when one of us matriculates. Where would they be without us? If they got too severe, we'd all go to Padua or someplace."

Wulf was completely ignorant of the politics of the colleges, and he really wasn't interested anyway. "Show me where the Louvre is," he demanded.

Mika called the students into a huddle, and they decided to retire to the Two Swords for a council of war.

"The landlord'll call the watch as soon as he catches sight of us!" Wulf protested.

"Nonsense," Mika said. "It's not always this crowded in the Quarter. For most of the year, he depends on us to buy ale. Some of us live there, in the upper rooms. Right now, he's fretting that we won't come back. To the Two Swords!"

Wulf sighed. He'd fallen among madmen and had to play their game.

As usual under such circumstances, Falcon awoke not knowing where he was. He scanned his surroundings with bleary eyes. He was in a dungeon, that was plain. But he had awakened in plenty of dungeons. Which one was this? Acre? No, it was too cold. Was he in Archbishop de Beaumont's clutches again? Not likely. Then he saw the man who lay snoring on the other side of the cell. He was a big man with a black mustache and he looked familiar. What was the name? Hugh de Chartres, that was it. Then the memories came flooding back: the tavern, the students, the tanners, the brawl. He groaned. After all the terrible battles and sieges he'd survived, to be thrown in the lockup for such a triviality!

He made a throbbing, crawling, painful journey to the other knight's side. He punched him, hoping the man wasn't in a death coma. He knew the dangers of too long a period of unconsciousness after a blow to the head. Hugh's snoring broke off and he sat up, rubbing his head. He looked at Falcon with perfectly clear eyes and smiled. "Good morning, Sir Draco. Fine battle, wasn't it? Where've they got us?" He looked around the cell with lively interest. Falcon snorted disgustedly. Obviously Hugh was one of those men who seem immune to the aftereffects of blows and hangovers.

"I've no idea," he answered.

"I'll bet it's the damned Louvre." He raised his voice to a piercing shout. "Jailer! Come here this instant!"

There was a shuffling noise outside and the face of an ugly, toothless old man appeared at the door's barred window. "What do you want?" said the jailer testily.

"I am Sir Hugh de Chartres. I am a knight of good birth and I am not to be treated in such a fashion. Bring me the warden of this place immediately."

"And I am Sir Draco Falcon. We were caught in a brawl by misfortune. I demand a hearing before my peers."

"Shut your knightly yaps," said the jailer. "You'll get your hearing in good time." Muttering to himself, the old man shuffled away.

"Well," said Hugh, "it was worth a try. Damn all jailers anyway. They were all whelped by the same bitch on the same dungheap."

The two settled down to await their fate. Experienced soldiers, they knew that there was little to do except sit and swap lies about their past exploits. Hugh, it seemed, was a professional tourney knight, who made a regular tour of the knightly events during the tourney season. He had made and lost several fortunes at various times. At the moment, he was down to one horse, his armor, and his weapons. He was hoping to recoup his losses in the Paris tourney and make enough to see him comfortably through the winter ahead, until spring saw the renewal of the season. He was almost as proud of his amatory prowess as of his fighting. By his own account he had sired bastards the length and breadth of Europe and was quite irresistible to peasant girls, abbesses, and high-born ladies alike.

Falcon made some mention of his own exploits in the Crusades, forbearing to mention that he had fought for both sides, told of being a galley slave and a prisoner in Palestine, and of the free band he now commanded. Hugh was interested in Falcon's new ideas of how to conduct a free war band.

"Sounds like a good life," Hugh commented. "None of this sitting around, twiddling your thumbs and waiting for your liege to make war on somebody. Not so chancy as tourneys, either. You say you pile all the loot together and share it out fairly?"

"Yes," Falcon answered, "according to a man's rank and time of service with the band. Any man caught withholding loot for himself is expelled immediately."

"A good idea, by God. I've seen too many victorious armies turn into squabbling mobs in fights over loot."

They were interrupted by the appearance of faces at the high window on the outer wall. "What have we here?" Falcon said. Then he recognized Mika and one of the other students from the night before.

"Are you well, Sir Draco?" said the Finn.

"Well enough, considering. Where's Wulf?"

"I'm standing on his shoulders," Mika answered.

"Now, about *The Analytics*," the other student said. "I've brought pen and ink and parchment, so if you'll just continue your lecture, I'll take notes and repeat your words to the others here."

"Aristotle!" yelled Falcon, outraged. "Not another word until you've gotten us out of here! It's your fault Hugh and I are trapped here when we've business elsewhere."

"I suppose he's right," said the student to Mika. "In any case, it would be easier if we could do this in a classroom someplace."

"Give us a few moments, Sir Draco," Mika said. "We have to see how much money we have. If we have enough for a bribe we'll have you out in a flash." The faces disappeared. Falcon sought deep within his soul for the strength to hold on to his temper. Mika reappeared. "Sir Draco," he said, "could you lend us ten florins?" Falcon groaned and buried his face in his hands.

Falcon sat back exhausted as the students completed their notes. Over the last three days they had drained him of his last remembered scraps of Aristotle. He swore to himself that if they asked him for Plato, he'd kill them all. They sat in the inn's saddle room above the stables, which the students had agreed to clean thoroughly, in return for its use as their classroom. Falcon found the strong stable smell infinitely preferable to the smells of the city outside. The cocks were beginning to crow as the sun rose and the church bells began to toll. The students started snuffing out the candle stubs they had bought from the church sexton.

Falcon had to admit to a grudging admiration for these students. At school, they led a rigorous existence. They were up before dawn to attend Mass and morning lectures, then after a bare few minutes for a bite to eat, had classes again until dark. Even after this exhausting schedule, their thirst for knowledge was such that they had sacrificed their precious few hours of sleep to attend his talks. Old Abraham would have been proud of them.

At the cathedral school, their studies were confined to the *trivium*—grammar, rhetoric, and logic—and to the *quadrivium*—arithmetic, geometry, astronomy, and music. These were the seven liberal arts, which supplemented the all-important study of theology and were in turn supplemented by the studies of law and medicine, the professions which required advanced study for higher degrees or church ordination. The subjects had changed little over the centuries, until a few decades before when scholars such as Peter Abelard had begun to break down the ancient, ossified routines of teaching by rote. Philosophy was a relatively new study, eyed with some disfavor by church authorities as conflicting with the established tenets of theology. To these students the thoughts of Aristotle came as a lavish banquet after a long diet of coarse bread and cheese.

The students got to their feet, yawning and stretching, massaging stiff joints. It was Sunday and at last they could get some sleep. Falcon also stood. Today he would exercise his horse and continue his so far fruitless search for the representative of the Viscount of Limoges.

"I don't know how we can ever repay you for this, Sir Draco," Mika said. "Or the ten florins either, for that matter."

"You'll manage," Wulf said. He had been sleeping on the straw during Falcon's lecture. "A pack of thieves like you should be able to come up with something."

"It won't be easy," Mika said. "Monday we begin a series of special lectures at the Temple and we'll be away all week."

"The Temple?" Falcon said. Something in his eye set alarm bells ringing in Wulf's head.

"Yes," Mika said. "We're all trooping off to the Temple to hear a series of talks by the warrior-monks on the doings in the Holy Land. The cathedral authorities think it'll be good for our souls. We'll use the time to go over our notes from these talks with you."

"Listen, Mika," Falcon said urgently, "get me into the Temple with you and you can forget about the ten florins."

"Leave the Temple alone, my lord," Wulf urged. "You've no business with them. Your business is here, in the city."

"You want to go to the Temple?" Mika said. "Whatever for?"

"My business is no concern of yours," Falcon answered. "Just get me inside and leave the rest to me."

"It should be no problem," Mika said. He was plainly fascinated at the prospect of taking part in some sort of intrigue. "We'll get you a student gown. Just keep the cowl up—you do look a bit elderly to be a student. Meet us outside the inn at daybreak Monday." The students left, happy to be relieved of their ten-florin obligation—money they would rather spend on wine and whores, in any case.

"This is ill advised, my lord," Wulf said. "You have no feud with the Temple. If Gerard were still alive, it'd be different, but he's dead and beyond your vengeance." Falcon had long suspected that Gerard de Ridemont, grand master of the Templars at the disastrous battle of Hattin, had taken part in the betrayal and death of his father.

"But we still don't know, Wulf," Falcon said passionately. "We don't know what Gerard was doing there that night, nor what part the new Temple has in the traitors' plans. If I can find out where the Temple records are kept, I may find something: where the other conspirators are, or even if Father is being kept somewhere."

"Your father is dead, Draco," Wulf said steadily. "Valdemar lied. Eudes was a powerful man, but no man could have survived what we saw that night."

As a boy, Falcon, in those days called Draco de Montfalcon, had been taken to the Crusade by his father, Eudes de Montfalcon. For reasons Falcon still didn't understand, Eudes had been taken prisoner and hideously tortured by his closest friends: the German knight Gunther Valdemar, the Flemish warrior-archbishop de Beaumont, the Englishman Nigel Edgehill, and Eudes's closest lifelong companion, Odo FitzRoy. Wulf, Falcon, and a Saracen horse handler had tried to rescue Eudes and had failed, the Saracen dying in the attempt. Their last sight of Eudes had been of his mutilated body, burned and bleeding, chained on the rack in Valdemar's castle of Hattin.

Falcon had dedicated his life to taking vengeance on the four. Three years before, he had caught up to Valdemar, but the German had tricked Falcon into killing him too quickly. With his dying breath, the German had told Falcon that Eudes was still alive, and that he, Valdemar, knew where Eudes was. Had it been the truth or merely a cruel lie, the final vengeance of a dying man?

There had been two other men at the castle that night. One was a Frankish knight that Falcon was almost sure was Gerard de Ridemont. The other was a Saracen emir whom Falcon suspected of being Malik en Nasr, the man all Crusaders knew by a corruption of his Arabic name: Saladin. These two mattered little now; both were dead. A few months before, Falcon had almost had de Beaumont in his grasp, but the man had escaped, though not before Falcon and his men had obliterated the hideous demonic sect he had assembled at a remote Alpine abbey. De Beaumont was a condemned heretic now, a hunted man throughout Christendom.

Falcon dragged his thoughts back to the present. "I have to know, Wulf. I'll never know rest until I know for certain."

"As you will, my lord," Wulf said. He knew better than to argue. "Will you take me with you to the Temple?"

"No, you could never pass as a student. Abraham couldn't even teach you your letters."

Wulf shrugged. He could never comprehend the

importance of reading. All the good poems were recited, and he would never trust words scratched on parchment. He needed to see a man's eyes and hear his voice to feel any sense of communication. "I'll follow behind, then, and camp in the woods near the Temple."

"That will be best," Falcon said. "Come on. Let's see to the horses."

That night, as so often in the last dozen years, the dreams came to Falcon. This time, he was back in the exercise yard at Suleiman's villa near Damascus. He was twenty-two years old, and he was sweating heavily as he slashed at a post with a long, curved, two-handed sword. It was a copy a smith had made of Suleiman's own sword, the incomparable Three Moons. The sword was of plain steel, unlike the Damascus of the original, and it was somewhat heavier. Suleiman, whose sons were dead, had promised to give Three Moons to Draco when he deemed the young man worthy.

Draco disengaged from his battle with the post to rest and drink some cool water from a gourd. The yard was full of men practicing, uttering the shrill war cries of the Saracen warrior. These were the men of Suleiman's personal guard. They fought with lances or swords and small round shields. Their swords were lighter than the Frankish ones. Most were straight, but many were of the new curved type, called a scimitar, which was just beginning to become popular in the East. All were wielded with one hand, the other holding a shield. In all the world, there was not another sword like Three Moons. To use the sword with both hands meant that the user had to forgo the protection of a shield, and this was beyond the skill of most men. Frankish knights sometimes swung their heavy swords with both hands as a desperation measure, but the swords were not designed for such use and the Frankish warriors were protected by armor far heavier than that worn by the Saracens.

Draco's gaze was caught by a flash of green, and he smiled. It was the green turban of Suleiman the Wise, the man Draco had come to love and respect more than any man since he had lost his father. The old man was crossing the yard, followed as always by his sword bearer, who carried the incomparable Three Moons. As always, Draco felt a near-worshipful swelling in his breast when he saw Suleiman. The famed teacher, magistrate, and soldier had rescued him from the living hell of a Turkish galley and in the years since had treated him as his own son.

The old man's face was sad, drawn, and pale, and Draco wondered what ill news Suleiman had received. He bowed deeply as Suleiman approached him. "Peace unto you, my father," Draco said formally.

"And unto you peace, my son," Suleiman answered. From outside, Draco could hear the sounds of wailing in the ritualized tones of Moslem mourning, and he suspected that this had something to do with Suleiman's expression. "I would speak to you, Draco, but first I must bring sad tidings to my men."

All had fallen silent at their lord's arrival, and they awaited his words respectfully.

"My people," Suleiman said in the high, singsong voice of a muezzin, "Islam is desolated and the faithful have lost the greatest among them. Salah-ed-Din, our great Malik en Nasr, is no more! His shield was the great wall of his people, and his sword was the terror of their enemies! To the poor he was a river of gold, and to the wicked he was the scourge of Allah! The greatest heart among us has broken at last, and the seas cannot hold the tears we shall shed!"

So that was it. The great and terrible Saladin was dead at last. All around the yard, men were falling to their knees, wailing and weeping. They ripped their garments and took up handfuls of dust to cast over their heads in token of mourning. The strange thing was that the mourning in Christendom would be nearly as great. The Crusaders had loved Saladin as a peerless knight and chivalrous foe more than they had hated him as the enemy of all Christians. Suleiman turned his sad face to Draco.

"I will not be a hypocrite and say that I am sorry," Draco said, "but I mourn for your people, who have lost their greatest leader. God give his soul peace."

"I know what it costs you to say that, my son," Suleiman said, "but I cannot share your suspicions. Salah-ed-Din was too noble a soul to have had part in that treacherous affair. You know that I have made many inquiries in your behalf, and nowhere can I find confirmation that he was at that castle on that terrible night."

"But, my father," Draco said, "he was above all things the servant of his people. To serve them, might he not have lowered himself to consorting with traitors? Would you not, if it was for the good of your people?" Draco said the words gently, something he was not accustomed to doing.

Suleiman's head bowed until his beard touched his breast. "I never thought to hear myself lectured in such matters by a Frankish boy, but I acknowledge the wisdom of your words. Yes, these evil times in which we live can corrupt the most virtuous." He looked up at the towering young man. "And now we must go and see to his burial. Even as we speak, the body of Salah-ed-Din lies before the Great Mosque of Damascus. You have chosen to remain a Christian, my son, but you are one of us, also. Will you come with us to bury him?"

Draco thought for a long moment, then: "I will come, my father. Let us bury him with all the honor due the greatest and wisest of men."

FIVE

It took from daybreak till almost midday for the student cortege to wend its weary way to the Temple. During that time, Falcon remained silent, reviewing in his mind all he knew of the Templars. He knew that the order had been founded nearly a century before by knights who pledged themselves to protect pilgrims in the Holy Land on their travels. They had received a charter from the Pope to form a monastic order. They became, in effect, monks in armor.

They had been glorious warriors in those days: monks who were ready at all times to leave their prayers and seize their swords. They had lived under a strict rule of chastity, poverty, and obedience. They had inspired the admiration of all Christendom.

The corruption had begun with that admiration. To the order had come lavish gifts of land and treasure, and the Templars had grown rich. Kings had given them funds to build great castles near the centers of power. The Temple at Paris and that at London were among the strongest castles in Christendom. Great nobles and monarchs had taken to depositing their treasuries in the Temple, since no rival would dream of attacking it. The Temple became, in effect, an enormous international banking institution. The days of the simple bands of warrior-monks were left far behind.

Now that the Crusader kingdoms overseas were being inexorably reduced, the power of the Templars in the Holy Land was nearly gone. Instead, they were becoming an ever-growing force in the politics of Europe.

The Templars had a rival order, the Knights of the Hospital of Jerusalem. As their title implied, the Hospitalers had begun as lay volunteers who had cared for the sick and injured among the pilgrims of the Holy Land. The unsettled times had caused them, too, to take up arms. Unlike the Templars, the Hospitalers had never sought wealth, and as far as Falcon knew they had kept their honor stainless. The Templars regarded them with barely concealed hostility.

Their first sign of the Temple was its battlements, looming above the surrounding forest. Then the walls came into view. Falcon was impressed. The towering inner keep was surrounded by a high wall consisting of a large number of round towers connected by curtain walls. The towers were spaced with care so that should an enemy gain the top of the wall, he would still come under fire of the two flanking towers, whose missile ranges overlapped. In effect, it was a complex of castles of varying sizes connected by walls. The main gate was flanked and topped by a fortress only slightly smaller than the great keep.

Professionally, Falcon tried to calculate how he

would go about taking such a place. He had to admit that he and his band alone could not. It would take the resources of a king to besiege the Temple, and then it would be starvation, not storm, that must reduce it. An attack on such defenses would be too costly. The only other answer was treachery from within. And whatever the Templars' faults, no member of the Temple had ever been known to betray the order. Falcon reflected on the foolishness of kings who would allow such castles to be built within their domains.

The students filed through the great fortified gateway. Beyond the huge triple portcullis was a long, dark corridor, pierced with spy holes in walls and ceiling. These were called murder holes, and a better name could not have been chosen for them. In the gate and on the battlements stood men with spears, wearing white robes with red crosses over their mail. Falcon knew these to be not the common footmen who carried out such duties at most castles, but knights of good blood. Even within his own little army, Falcon had difficulty persuading his men of knightly rank to carry out the duties of routine soldiering, but the warrior-monks always obeyed without question. He had to admire such superb discipline.

A man in the white robes of the order met the students when they emerged into the bailey, a wide space of grassy ground that separated the great keep from the outer walls. The bailey was filled with wooden structures such as stables and blacksmith workshops, but left plenty of open ground for practice in warlike games and for pasturing the animals in time of siege. He noted with reluctant approval that all the wooden structures were built so that they could be quickly knocked apart and stored within the keep when under attack. This guarded against fire and denied cover to any enemy who might get past the outer defenses.

"Welcome to the Paris Temple," said the white-robed man. "The authorities of your school have graciously granted that we Templars be allowed to teach you students some things about Christ's work abroad. This is fitting, for just as we defend the faith with our swords, so you young men must defend it with your learning."

It was excellent flattery, and Falcon had to award the man points for astuteness. The students were nothing if not vain, and he was playing upon that vanity masterfully.

"Come with me," the Templar said, "and I shall show you your quarters for the next week. Then there will be a meal in the great hall and after that the first of your lectures."

The students were led to a large, spacious dormitory. It was a single long room with its walls lined with bunks. These were wooden bedframes with woven-leather straps supporting straw-stuffed pallets. There were washbasins and candle sconces, and the floor was covered with fresh straw. Otherwise the room was bare. It was a severe and Spartan arrangement, but it was better than the students were used to in the squalor and overcrowding of the Paris slums.

After leaving their meager possessions next to their beds, the students were taken to the hall. Falcon, looking out from raised cowl, took stock of his surroundings. They were passing through an exquisitely carved cloister when something out of the ordinary caught his eye.

Standing outside a door opening off the cloister was a small group of people who obviously did not belong to the Temple. One had the look of a senior steward to a good household, and two others were servingmen of standard type, but it was the fourth member of the little group who stood out like a stained-glass window in a border fort.

First of all, she was a woman, and the Templars seldom allowed women within their sanctuaries. This spoke well of the lady's family connections. Second, she was extraordinarily beautiful. Her hair was invisible beneath her coif and wimple, but her face was a fetching triangle with fine small features and huge brown eyes. Her gown was in the latest fashion, skintight from the hips upward, and it displayed a perfect figure. What on earth is she doing here? Falcon wondered.

The woman eyed the students as they passed, and Falcon read her expression as one of anger and frustration. Whatever she had come here for, the Templars had given her no satisfaction.

The students crossed the bailey to the great central keep. This massive pile of stone was if anything even more formidable than the outer walls. They climbed a wooden stairway to a small door on the second story of the keep. There were no entrances on the ground level. Should an enemy gain the bailey, the defenders need merely go into the keep and knock away the stair in order to be secure. The small door on the second story with its overhanging murder holes was immune from assault.

The great hall was an enormous room that extended for almost the full area of one floor. The windows were narrow arrow slits that admitted little light, but the whitewashed walls and ceiling brightened it somewhat. Its floor was covered with long tables made of boards laid atop trestles, and the Templars were just seating themselves for their meal.

From a high pulpit upon one wall a chaplain was intoning grace. He would continue readings from the

Bible or from various theologians throughout the meal. In other castles, there would be dogs tussling on the floor and jugglers, singers, and tumblers entertaining the diners. Here all was monastic and severe. Falcon wondered whether the gathering would be so decorous if there were no strangers present.

The meal was equally monastic in its plainness, but it was plentiful, as befitted men who might at any time have to don heavy mail and fight and who in any case had to spend part of each day in strenuous training for war. Besides the inevitable black bread and cheese, there were broiled fish fresh-caught from the river, hard-boiled eggs, strips of grilled venison supplied by the Temple's huntsmen, and bowls of fresh greens. Although the quality of the food was excellent, it was prepared without spices and only the slightest trace of salt. The students, accustomed to living for long periods on thin rations and observing the church's frequent fast days, fell to with the appetite of men never certain of their next meal.

Falcon was likewise eating heartily when he noticed a Templar watching him with more than passing interest. Immediately, Falcon was apprehensive. Had the man seen his face, and did he know him? He was sure that he had not let his cowl back far enough to expose his face. What was the fellow looking at? He followed the path of the man's gaze. His hands! He'd forgotten how distinctive his own hands were. They were deeply tanned and bore many scars, and they were heavily callused from his years on the galley and from a lifetime of working with weapons. They were definitely not the hands of a student, and there was no way a seasoned warrior like this would mistake them for such. He thought feverishly to come up with a cover story.

"Your pardon, young man," the Templar said at

66

length, "but you seem not to have the aspect of a student. You look more like a warrior."

"You are perceptive, sir," Falcon said. "Indeed, from my youngest days, I trained to be a knight. As a squire, I accompanied King Philip's army to the Crusade. When I saw how the kings all bickered among themselves, each more interested in seizing glory and riches for himself than in rescuing the Holy Sepulcher, I knew that Christendom needed more than strong arms. Then I was struck with a terrible illness in Palestine, and I swore a holy oath that should God spare me, I would return home and study to become a doctor of theology. Even though I was beyond the usual age to take up these studies, I have persevered and will soon have my degree."

"Admirable," said the Templar. "Christendom stands in need of learned men. God knows that there are more than enough warriors to go around. And your name, sir?"

"Drogo de Caen." This was the name he and the students had agreed upon.

"From Normandy?"

"Yes," Falcon said. In truth, Falcon's family lands were in Normandy near Caen, although he had not been home in nearly twenty years. He was sticking as close to the truth as he could. The Templar asked no more questions, but Falcon was fairly sure that he had not heard the last of this matter.

After the meal they were given an hour to stroll about the grounds before their first lectures began. Falcon kept to the deep shade of the cloister, hoping that he would not be noticed, but it was not his lucky day for unobtrusiveness. He heard a throat being cleared behind him, and he turned. To his surprise, it was the lady he'd seen earlier. She was smaller than she had seemed at first, somewhat under five feet. It was her noble bearing that had made her seem taller.

"I beg your pardon, sir," she said. "You do not belong to the Temple, do you?" Her manner was the courteous but cool one adopted by the wellborn when not sure of the addressee's station.

"I do not, my lady," Falcon admitted. "I am a student, here to attend a series of lectures. May I be of assistance?" Unconsciously, he had addressed her in courtly French, rather than the rough soldier's patois he usually used, or the half-Latin hybrid tongue that students employed. The language of the wellborn seemed to set the lady at ease.

"My name is Isabeau de Clare. I am here to see a—a friend, but the Templars tell me that it is not permitted."

"That is odd," Falcon remarked. "I knew they lived under a vow of chastity, but I would think that visiting between friends would be permitted."

"They say it is because he is about to take his final vows, and he must not be distracted from his meditations."

"Ah," Falcon said. "And this man's name?" He was almost certain that he knew already.

"Claude de Coucy. Sir, if you are permitted inside the keep, is it possible that you might deliver a message for me?"

Falcon smiled to himself. It was indeed the young knight he had met on the road to Paris. "I will try, my lady." This might be amusing.

"Please tell him that Isabeau waits for him at the inn called the Griffin. It is on the road between here and Paris."

"I know the place. We passed it on our way here this morning. Is there anything else?"

"Tell him I *must* see him before he takes his final

vows." Impulsively, she seized his hand and kissed it. "Oh, thank you, sir. But whom am I thanking?"

"Drogo de Caen, my lady, a poor student of theology." She studied what she could see of his face beneath the cowl with a look of doubt. I can't even fool this child, Falcon thought. I should never have come here.

She looked down at the rock-hard hands she was holding. "Drogo, then. Please help me, sir."

"I'll do what I can, lady. And now, perhaps it is best that we not be seen together." Isabeau released his hands and rejoined her party. Falcon smiled to himself. So, young Claude's lady love had followed him to the Temple to make a last, desperate bid for him before she lost him forever to the Temple. It was not Falcon's habit to meddle in other people's personal lives, but doing the Temple a bad turn would not disturb his conscience at all. Quite the contrary, in fact. He'd see what he could do to make the young fool see the error of his ways and return home to breed a pack of young de Coucys with this fetching little lady.

The first of the lectures was as thunderously boring as Falcon's worst fears had foretold. There was endless dwelling upon the glories of the Templars' exploits in the Holy Land, most of them having taken place so long ago as to be nearly forgotten. To hear them tell it, Falcon thought, one would think that the order could take sole credit for all Christian victories in the Holy Land. The students were paying little attention, but were vigorously swapping notes about Aristotle or their girlfriends. Falcon stood it as long as he could, then he rose and left the lecture room. No one appeared to notice.

He found himself in one of the long cloisters that seemed to connect all parts of the castle. Along one side was a wall pierced with the entrances to rooms. Along the other stretched a delicate tracery of stonework through which could be seen a pleasant garden. Head down, Falcon walked along the cloister to see where it led him.

He was stopped by a white-robed man who looked suspicious. "You there, where are you going? Should you not be with the visiting students?"

"Your pardon, sir," Falcon said. "I have lately been afflicted with a flux of the bowels and had to take my leave temporarily."

"Oh," said the knight, mollified. "There's a jakes down there." He pointed to the end of the cloister. "Past the St. Mary chapel." Falcon thanked him and went in the indicated direction. As he passed the entrance of the chapel he glanced inside and was met with an unusual sight. A man lay on the floor before the altar, dressed in white with arms outstretched as if he were crucified. Falcon could only see his back and the back of his head, which was covered with close-cropped hair of a sandy hue.

Falcon looked about. The cloister seemed empty. He entered the chapel and approached the prone figure. No doubt of it, this was Claude de Coucy. "Claude?" Falcon said.

"Go away," Claude said. "I must not be disturbed in these final hours of my vigil."

"I have a message for you, Claude," Falcon said. The young knight looked up in exasperation, then in astonishment.

"Sir Draco! What are you doing here?" The side of his face was smudged from being pressed against the cold stone floor.

"I've come to bring you a message from Isabeau de Clare."

"Isabeau!" Claude sprang to his feet with an eagerness that boded ill for his vow of chastity, not to mention that of obedience. "How did you encounter her? I had thought her long gone from my life."

"At this moment, she resides in an inn called the Griffin, a few miles from here. She has been trying to see you, but the Templars would not allow it, so she asked me to tell you that she wants to meet with you before you make your final vows."

"And you came here disguised as a student just to tell me!" Claude said. "How can I thank you?"

"Well—" Falcon said, shrugging. "Consider it the favor of one knight to another. Brotherhood of chivalry, you understand."

"And those others with me said you were a mere sell-sword. How wrong they were."

Falcon spread his hands as if mystified at the unprovoked hostility of his fellow man.

"Ah, but how can I see her?" Claude agonized. "I am not permitted to leave here."

"We could spirit you out in a student robe," Falcon proposed.

"But if I were caught!" Claude protested. "My brothers would expel me from the order and I would never be permitted my final vows!"

"If you are so intent on taking those vows," Falcon pointed out, "they why are you so anxious to see Isabeau?"

"You are right," admitted Claude, looking hangdog. "I must not be truly sure of my vocation. I have loved Isabeau since we were little more than children. It was always our dream to marry someday."

Falcon contemplated this extreme oddity. According to the accepted rules of chivalry, one was supposed to worship some unattainable female, preferably one married to somebody else. One was *never* supposed to love one's own wife, nor to marry for

71

love. The knightly class married only for political or economic advantage. This must be some new wrinkle the poets hadn't discovered yet.

"Whatever the state of your soul," Falcon said, "she's at the Griffin. Will you see her, vows or no vows?"

Claude struggled with himself for at least a half second. "Yes! Take me to her!"

"Good, then," Falcon said, clapping him on the shoulder. "Meet me by the main gate at midnight, out of sight of the guards. I'll have a student robe for you."

"How will we get past the guards?" Claude asked.

"I'll think of something. I usually do. Now, lie back down and murmur prayers to the floor." Claude complied, and Falcon left the chapel.

He continued his explorations. He asked a lay worker the location of the master's chambers, and a door was pointed out to him. He tested it. It swung slightly open. There seemed to be nobody in the first room he saw, so he stepped silently inside. The room was small, and in one corner beneath a window there was a writing stand with quill and ink. This was the scriptorium, and therefore the chests lying about probably contained the Temple's written records. He tried one. Locked. He tried the others. All locked. He cursed mentally. Had he undertaken this dangerous mission merely to aid a lovesick young fool? Then he heard voices from another of the chambers. Delicately he tiptoed to a door that was open just a crack.

In the next room, men were discussing something with no slight urgency. He was having difficulty making out the words, but he was well acquainted with the tones of men holding a council of war or a conspiracy, and that was how these men sounded.

There were at least three speaking. The subject

seemed to be murder. Just who was to be murdered was a mystery, because the men were using some sort of code in their speech.

"—Le Rouge is finally dead. With Sans-Terre in his place, we are now in a strong position." This was the voice of a fairly old man, but it was powerful. Le Rouge? Falcon thought. Sans-Terre? The red one and the landless one? Who were they talking about? He ceased speculating and resumed listening.

"Le Grand can thwart us," said another. "His power grows daily. We must do something about him."

"That will require the consent of the grand master of the order," said a third.

"He will be here soon, perhaps within the week," said the first. "We must delay our decision until then." There were signs that the meeting was breaking up, and Falcon stepped to the outer door and opened it. The men came through the door at which he had been listening, and Falcon swung the other door shut behind him as if he had just come in. The oldest of the Templars regarded him coldly. "Yes? What is it?"

"Your pardon, sir. One of my fellow students is ill, and he may need to return to Paris before morning. If I might have a pass for him and myself, it would spare having to disturb you should he need to leave tonight."

"I would advise against it, young man," said the old Templar, who was obviously the castellan here. As governor or warden of the castle, arrivals and departures were part of his responsibilities. "The roads are not safe after dark. Two men, one of them ill, would be easy prey. Best wait until morning."

"I think we need not worry about this one," said another of the Templars. Falcon saw that it was the

73

knight who had questioned him in the great hall. "I spoke with him this afternoon. He is a soldier, and has fought in Palestine."

"A Crusader, eh?" said the master, unbending a little.

"Yes, my lord. I have taken up studies in fulfillment of a vow."

"You should be safe enough, then. The riffraff hereabouts are no danger to a trained man. Have you a sword?"

"Yes, my lord."

"Very well, then." The master took an old sheet of parchment and scribbled a few words upon it. More important, he poured hot wax on the parchment and impressed it with his seal ring. Even if the gate guard could not read, he would know his master's seal. Falcon took the parchment and left the room with a profound sense of relief.

He returned to the students' quarters and sat on a pallet pondering what he'd heard. Who were these Templars planning to do away with? Not that it was any concern of his. People were always plotting murder. The higher one was on the social scale, the more frequently were differences settled by assassination. Still, he was intrigued.

Le Rouge, Sans-Terre, Le Grand—who might they be? Sans-Terre, now: The English sometimes called their new king John Lackland, because when the Old King had divided up his lands among his older sons, there had been none left for John. If King John was Sans-Terre, then Le Rouge would have to be Richard. Richard's hair had been red, so the name would fit. And if that was the case, then Le Grand, the great one, would have to be—a sudden sweat appeared on Falcon's brow. Le Grand could only be Philip Augustus, the King of France himself!

Falcon's mind spun and darted, examining the ramifications of this thought. Surely the Temple was over-reaching itself, to plot the death of a king. Then he reminded himself of old Abraham's exercises in rigorous logic. Pay attention only to facts, not to feelings. Carefully, he considered everything he knew about the situation. At the end of his analysis, he had to admit that there was nothing illogical in such a plot.

He knew that the Temple's main advantage lay in its being a powerful, stable, international order. It battened upon the weakness of the temporal monarchs and papacy. One look at this castle had told Falcon that no king with his wits about him would allow such a strongpoint within his kingdom if he did not command its allegiance.

The greatest threat to the Temple's preeminence was a strong king, Pope, or emperor. Just now there was no emperor. The new Pope was a good one, but he had inherited such a shambles of a church from his predecessors that he would need many years of house-cleaning before he could begin to take an active part in politics outside it. He might die of old age long before he finished his work.

That left the kings. There were few kings of any power within Christendom. Germany and Italy were a welter of petty kingdoms, principalities, arch-bishoprics, and the holdings of various barons. Spain was a world of its own beyond the Pyrenees, and absorbed in its own unending wars between Christian and Moor. England's king was now John Plantagenet, the weakling. Poland, Hungary, and Russia were too remote to consider.

Only King Philip of France had power and prestige to match the Temple. He had a long struggle ahead to consolidate his inheritance, but he seemed to be a man who could accomplish it. Falcon's life had been spent in the fields of war, in Palestine and in a Turkish slave galley, not in the polished courts of Europe. Nevertheless, even he could see that the Temple, the papacy, and the throne of France were on a collision course.

SIX

FALCON LURKED in a dark corner of the wall near the main gate. There were torches set in sconces flanking the gate, and in their light he could see a couple of sleepy sentries standing with glaives as their captain walked back and forth to keep himself awake. Night guard was always one of the greatest miseries of the military profession.

He heard someone approach. The man was feeling his way along a wall, trying not to trip. "Claude?" Falcon whispered.

"Here," said the figure. "Where are you?"

Falcon reached out and grasped an arm, pulling Claude into the angle he'd found. "Put this on," Falcon ordered, thrusting the student robe into Claude's hands. Luckily, one of the more fastidious scholars had brought along a change of clothes and Falcon had bribed him out of it.

Claude scrambled into the robe, getting the unfamiliar garment on backward on the first try, then righting it.

"Now," Falcon whispered urgently, "lean on me. You're sick, remember?"

Arms around each other's shoulders, the two lurched toward the gate. Claude began to mutter as if delirious. "Easy," Falcon said. "You're supposed to be sick, not incapacitated. How'll they believe you can walk back to Paris?" Claude straightened somewhat as the guard captain came to investigate.

"My comrade is ill," Falcon said. "I have come to take him to his home in Paris, where he can be cared for."

"Have you a pass?" the captain asked. Falcon held out the parchment. The man took it and walked over to the torches. Slowly and haltingly, he began to read the message aloud. Literacy, even if only partial, was far more common among the Templars than in secular society. " 'These—two'—ah—'men,' " the captain said, " 'have—my'—ah, I guess that's 'permission'—'to'—ah—'pass—through—the—gate.' " The art of silent reading was unknown. The captain peered closely at the seal until he was satisfied. "Everything seems in order," he said, then, to the other guards, "Open the port."

They unbolted and opened a tiny door within the main gate, and by dint of much stooping and squeezing Falcon and Claude forced their way out into the open. There was enough moonlight for faint illumination, so they were careful to keep up a slow, staggering gait as long as they were within possible eyesight of the castle, then they strode briskly down the road. They were startled by a sound of hooves, and then a man, mounted and leading another horse, drew even with them.

"You weren't in there long," Wulf said.

"There was no need," Falcon answered. "You

remember Claude, don't you? He's riding with us part-way back to Paris. Claude, you can ride double with Wulf."

"Ride double?" Claude said doubtfully. "It seems unknightly."

Falcon laughed. "Claude, you definitely are not the stuff of which Templars are made."

Unseen in the darkness, Claude was flushing with mortification. He had forgotten that the great seal of the Temple depicted two knights riding a single horse, in token of their vow of poverty. He scrambled up behind the Saxon.

They rode slowly, for no horse is at its best carrying double. The moon was almost down when they reached the Griffin. Claude alit and pounded on the door of the inn. There were noises from inside as someone arose to open up.

"Are you coming in, Sir Draco?" Claude asked.

"We have business in Paris," the knight answered.

"Then, go with all my thanks," Claude said. Then: "But how shall I get back into the Temple?"

"Your problem," Falcon replied. "I agreed to try to get you out, not in."

Through the rest of the night, Falcon and Wulf made their easy way toward Paris. There was no sense in rushing, because the gates would not be opened until sunrise. On the way, Falcon told Wulf of his adventures in the Temple. He said that he had failed in his attempt to find out about his father, but that he had uncovered a conspiracy.

"What of it, my lord?" Wulf said. "What do you have except some half-heard words in terms meant to confuse?"

"But think, Wulf," Falcon said, "this is a conspiracy to murder a king!"

Wulf shrugged. "We've seen dead kings before. After two days, they smell much like other men."

"Wulf," Falcon said, "consider: A king, apprised of such a plot, is in a position to reward the appriser more generously than other men."

"Isn't there a saying about the gratitude of princes? As I recall, it isn't considered desirable."

"I don't plan to ask for any long-term favors, Wulf. A simple, quick cash reward will be quite sufficient."

They were at the Two Swords in time for breakfast, and the landlord had laid out hot rolls and cold meat pies for the guests. Hugh was already seated at a table, crumbs dropping from his mustache. "Where've you been, Sir Draco?" Hugh asked.

"I had to leave the city for a while," Falcon said, picking up a meat pie and biting into it. Wulf ripped a loaf of bread in two and spread butter on it. A serving girl brought a pitcher of hot spiced wine that gave off a fragrant steam.

When they were full, Falcon leaned back against a wall and spoke to Hugh. "Sir Hugh, when will the tourney begin?"

"In three days, if the weather is good," the knight replied. "Changed your mind about taking part?"

"I've been thinking about it," Falcon said.

"Splendid!" Hugh said. "Come with me today. I'll be going to the tourney ground to exercise my horse. You'll need to learn the ground, and you'll see many of the others there. Some very illustrious knights are taking part."

"First, I need to get some sleep," Falcon said. "I've been out all night."

"Seeing a lady, eh?" Hugh said, winking and giving

Falcon an elbow that would have broken most men's ribs.

"Something like that," Falcon replied.

"A tourney!" Wulf protested, when they were alone again. "Why take part in such foolishness? You've said yourself that you have more important business here. You've already let yourself be distracted from that business too long."

"Silence, Wulf," Falcon muttered. "You're as bad as a wife."

"And why not?" Wulf asked. "Tourneys are foolishness, as I said and as you know. You've seen them. Some idiot goes out to do battle for the honor of his lady fair. She gives him a kerchief to tie around his arm as a favor. The next thing you know, he's had ten feet of ash pole as thick as your wrist shoved through his belly. She sheds a few pretty tears. Before the tourney's over, a dozen other fools have worn her kerchief. You've never taken part in such idiocy before, so why now? If we were desperate, I could understand, but we're not. The chance of some ransom money is not worth the risk."

Falcon was on his knees, dumping his fighting gear from the oiled leather bags he kept it all in. He looked up at the Saxon in exasperation. "In the first place, I'm not taking part for the money. I'm doing it to distinguish myself and catch the king's eye."

"Oh, the king's eye, is it? You still hope to warn him of this plot? Why don't you just go knock on his door?"

"Wulf," Falcon said slowly, "you don't just knock on the door and say: 'I'd like to see the king, please.' It's just not done."

"I've seen you do it before," Wulf retorted. "And successfully, too."

"Not here," Falcon said. "France isn't Palestine. They're civilized here. You have to kill a few people to gain the king's notice." Falcon shook out his mailshirt and began examining it minutely. "Besides, that's not what's bothering you. You're angry because you won't be able to fight by my side, as usual."

"It's not fair!" Wulf fumed. "Why are only the wellborn permitted to slaughter one another in a tourney? It's not that way on the battlefield! Just because I'm baseborn and a Saxon is no reason I shouldn't accompany you as I always do."

"Your being a Saxon has nothing to do with it," Falcon said. "And for that matter, you are wellborn, if breeding alone is of any account."

"There've been no wellborn Saxons these last hundred and thirty or so years," Wulf said bitterly. "We're all peasants or serfs now, ever since William and his Normans disinherited us."

"Too bad," Falcon said. "If men can't defend their land they should be grateful that they're given any to work, even if they can't own it!" Wulf had forgotten for the moment that Draco was a Norman.

"And work it so that our knightly lords can butcher one another for play!"

"Enough of this!" Falcon shouted, hurling the now-empty oiled bag at Wulf's face. "You'll be my attendant in the tourney. If I'm unhorsed you can run in and pull me out before I'm captured. That much is permitted. If you have to dagger a few to get me out, well, tourneys are pretty confused affairs. Probably no one will notice."

"I still don't like it," Wulf maintained sullenly.

"Nobody is asking you to," Falcon said.

The tourney ground was a large open field overlooked by the city walls. Nearby were numerous houses and shops, for overcrowded Paris was spilling out of its walls and people were willing to endure the insecurity of dwelling without the walls for the sake of greater space and cheap land.

The periphery of the field was crowded with the colorful pavilions of the knights who would be participating. Before each tent was propped the owner's shield, brightly painted with his personal device. Heralds were wandering about noting down the knights' arms on long rolls of parchment.

On the field, a quintain had been set up for the riders to practice with. It consisted of an upright post with a pivoted crossbar atop it. On one end of the crossbar was a miniature shield. From the other dangled a heavy sandbag. It took adroit lancework to strike the shield fairly and at the same time avoid being clouted by the sandbag. It was one of the first exercises given a new squire, and one of the most hated, but even the most experienced knights practiced at it almost daily in times of peace.

Falcon tried the quintain a few times to limber up and give his horse some exercise. On his first two tries, his lance point struck the little shield at least four inches off center, and he knew that he was badly out of practice. He concentrated upon precision of aim until he was striking the center every time.

As he trotted away from the quintain, a knight rode up to him. He recognized Hugh's bristling mustache. Hugh's shield was painted with vertical stripes of white and green. In the lore of heraldry, the white stood for silver, since silver gilding was far too costly to use on a shield. The man was dressed in heavy mail with long sleeves that extended to cover the hands in iron mittens with leather palms. The fronts of his legs were protected by long strips of mail that tied in back.

"Good day, Sir Draco." Hugh ran an expert eye over Falcon's mount and equipment. "That hauberk's Saracen work, isn't it?" he asked.

"It is," Falcon replied.

"Do you have another to fight in? I think that's the finest mail I've ever seen. Every knight here will be trying to capture you so they can lay hands on it."

"Damn!" Falcon said. He hadn't thought of that. "Won't there be a set rate for ransoming our arms and mounts?"

"There will be," Hugh said, "but if something like that fell into my hands, I'd be away before the man I'd won it from woke up."

"Well," Falcon said, "I'll have to arrange something."

"Would you care to try a few sword strokes?" Hugh asked.

"Gladly," Falcon answered. Hugh had a pair of practice swords made of whalebone, which was tough and would not splinter like wood. They were weighted to heft like the real swords they represented. In the tourney, sharp battle weapons would be used.

Falcon donned his helmet and tied its chin cord. "You won't be using that helmet, will you?" Hugh said.

"Why not?" Falcon asked.

"It's outdated. It gives your face no protection. You should get one like mine." Hugh took his helm from his saddlebow. It was round-topped, and the bowl came down far enough to cover the ears. The front dipped lower to cover the face with an iron mask, pierced with holes for sight and breath. Like his shield, it was painted in white and green stripes.

"You're half blind and deaf in one of those," Falcon retorted. "I like to see and hear what's around me when I fight, and I don't like to suffocate in the meantime."

"It's better than getting a lance through your face," Hugh said. He clapped the helm over his mail coif and seated it firmly.

"If you use your shield well, your face is protected," Falcon said.

"Eh?" Hugh's voice came faintly through the breathing holes.

"Oh, never mind," Falcon said.

"Eh?"

They traded blows from horseback for a while, and Falcon found Hugh to be extremely strong and skillful with both sword and shield. Many very powerful men neglected shieldwork in order to overwhelm an adversary with sheer fury, but Hugh fought with careful cunning, and that pleased Falcon. Both were very solicitous of their horses. It would be disastrous to have a horse lamed before the tourney.

Feeling sufficiently exercised, the two rode from the field, well satisfied with the practice. They'd given each other a hard workout, but neither had shown the other his favorite moves. Friendship went only so far. There was no guarantee they would not be facing each other over shield rims sometime during the tourney.

Hugh pulled off his helm, and a cloud of steam arose from its interior. His face was red and sweaty. He scanned the surrounding tents, casting an eye over the various arms displayed. "Roger de Burgh's here," Hugh said. "He's a cunning fighter. And there's de Mortimer. He's a fine horseman, and watch out for his lance. He has a trick of feinting high to draw your shield, then going in low to your right and catching you in the side. I've seen him gut three men that way." Hugh went on for some time, describing the various participants and naming their particular tricks or styles of fighting. Hugh was an expert of long experience on the tourney circuit, and Falcon knew that he could not have fallen in with a more valuable companion.

They were standing leaning on their shields when they were approached by two heralds. "Good day, Sir Hugh," one said. He then turned to Falcon. "Sir Hugh, of course, is familiar to us, but we cannot seem to find your arms in our rolls." He eyed Falcon's shield. "Argent, a falcon sable displayed, in her talons holding thunderbolts azure. The blazoning seems in order." Heralds were forever dreaming up complicated, niggling little rules to regulate their craft. "Your name, sir?"

"Sir Draco Falcon, late of Palestine."

"Ah, a Crusader. There are many here. By whom were you knighted?"

"By Raymond of Tripoli."

"The Prince of Galilee! Were there witnesses? Forgive me, sir, but there are many impostors who pose as true knights."

"None now alive," Falcon answered.

"Well, no matter," the herald said. "Anyone can see that you are what you claim. You are now entered upon the rolls of heraldry. Within a year or two, your arms will be blazoned upon the rolls of all the heralds in Christendom."

"I thank you, sirs," Falcon said. The heralds took their leave ceremoniously.

"Silly buggers," said Hugh. "Act as if they're as important as knights. Now they're saying they can expel a knight from all tourneys if he doesn't follow all their damned little rules."

"Give men a little authority," Falcon said, "and

they'll turn it into real power. Let them keep their power long enough, and they'll make it hereditary."

"Damn all heralds, anyway," Hugh said. He spat at a passing chicken and struck it squarely in the eye.

Wulf arrived with a basket filled with food he had bought from the vendors who swarmed all about. They sat on the ground and devoured sausages and meat pastries and passed a skin of wine from hand to hand. Falcon eyed his battered shield dubiously. "Wulf, take my shield to a painter and have the colors redone. I want to make a good show when the tourney starts."

"Good idea," Hugh commented. "Don't want them to think you're hiding."

"Hugh," Falcon said, "do you know of a man who's been taking ransoms steadily, lately?"

"Several. Why?"

"Take me to one."

They located a knight named Chrétien de Monteil. With a little questioning, they established that, yes, he had in his possession three hauberks he had won in recent months. The former owners had been unable to ransom them, and he had been unable to sell them as yet. He agreed to lend one of them to Falcon for a small fee. If it was lost, Falcon would have to ransom it back, but the cost would be nowhere near the value of his own armor.

Falcon tried on his new gear. It was old-fashioned in design, with wide sleeves only to the elbows, and the skirts extended only to mid-thigh. That suited Falcon, as larger dimensions would have made the garment uncomfortably heavy. As it was, it weighed nearly twice what Falcon's own armor did. It was a bit rusty, so Falcon had Wulf take it to one of the boys who were all about, earning pennies by polishing mail. They put the shirt into a barrel with sand and fine gravel, poured in a quart or two of vinegar, and rolled the barrel around for an hour or two. The mail emerged clean and sparkling as if new-made.

For the next two days Falcon haunted the tourney field. He observed all the knights at their practice, cold-bloodedly picking those who seemed to be his likeliest targets. Others were observing him as closely. He was careful to display knightly competence but no brilliance. Should he look too formidable, only true champions would seek him out in joust or melee. He would then be lucky to emerge with his life, let alone wealthier and in royal favor.

On the day before the tourney, a knight arrived with a sizable retinue. His shield bore the device of an eagle's head. He was a huge man on a towering horse, and there were six knights in his train.

"Rollo Dupré," Hugh said to Falcon. "Just our luck he's here. I've seen him at a score of tourneys. In the melee, he and his men will stand off to one side. As men grow tired, they'll rush in and snap up any that are easy prey."

"Is that permitted?" Wulf asked.

"Once the two sides join battle in the melee," Hugh said, "there are no rules. You try not to kill, because a dead man gives no ransom, and that's the only reason. Plenty die in any case. I've seen Rollo kill a dozen at least. Once he's fighting, he's like a madman."

"Steer clear of that one, my lord," Wulf said. It was a piece of advice Falcon did not need.

They watched Rollo practicing against other knights. He was not averse to trampling a fallen adversary, even in practice. His sword blows were so powerful that more than one shield cracked beneath them. On the day of the tourney, he would be using the long, heavy knightly blade, and not many would survive those blows.

While they lounged at the Two Swords, Hugh regaled them with stories of tourneys he had taken part in, of strategies he had learned by hard experience, of little tricks that gave a man a slight edge in battle. And battle it was. The tourney was a brutal miniature war, and had all the dangers of the battlefield except for the absence of arrows. In fact, it could be somewhat more dangerous, for in a true battle, the knights could while away much of the time slaughtering the enemy's foot soldiers at little danger to themselves. In the melee, on the other hand, it was solely a matter of hand-to-hand combat between horsemen equally armed.

As Hugh had said, once the fight was joined, there were no rules. Men would strike from behind, seek to injure an enemy's horse, or form groups to gang up on a single opponent. Sportsmanship was not even a concept. Men died of wounds, of suffocation, of heatstroke, and in falls. Trampling was common. "If you fall in the melee," Hugh said, "pretend you're a turtle and huddle under your shield. There're no enemy footmen, you see, so your main danger is from the horses. Above all, don't stand up until your man tells you it's safe, because someone will ax you in the head."

Tourneys were a relatively new phenomenon, only a generation or two old. They had begun as warlike exercises to keep the knights in fighting trim in the infrequent stretches of peace. Eventually, random challenges had become social events as it was discovered that these bloody get-togethers were a fine excuse for people to gather in one place to meet, gossip, play at politics, and generally have a good time. Then the new cult of chivalry had arisen and the tourney had become the focal point and rage of polite society, because tourneys were, above all else, knightly affairs.

Previously, the only excuse for the knightly class

had been the waging of war. Now, with chivalry and the tourneys, there was a whole social mystique to knighthood. Ladies could attend tourneys, unlike wars, and there was much romantic nonsense such as the Queen of Love and Beauty, and a mock storming of the Castle of Love, in which young knights attacked a small wooden fortress defended by ladies who pelted them with flowers. It was enough to turn the stomach of a serious soldier like Draco Falcon, but he could sympathize with the ladies. They had seized upon the cult of chivalry to turn the armored brutes they were married to into something resembling human beings. All over Christendom, knights were learning to read just so that they could send love poems to their ladies.

By now, tourneys were so popular that they were sponsored by kings, as this one was, in spite of the fact that they were splendid occasions for the nobles to get together and plot against royal authority. Crusaders had held tourneys during lulls in sieges, even though the practice was condemned by the church. The knighthood of Europe ignored the papal ban on tourneys with the same blasé disdain with which they regarded other religious proscriptions against their favored pastimes, such as the injunction against killing.

Thus far, Falcon had avoided all such knightly foolery, but on this occasion there was no way to back out. The stakes were just too high. It was a risk he was prepared to take.

SEVEN

THE MORNING of the first day of the tourney dawned bright and cloudless, in contrast to the previously gloomy weather. Falcon, Wulf, and Hugh had spent the night in a pavilion they had rented at an exorbitant rate in order to be spared having to rise early and then endure a ride through the thronged streets of Paris, possibly to arrive soaked with the morning's chamber-pot dumpings.

Early as it was, the tourney field was a pandemonium of hawkers and vendors, tumblers, whores, and cutpurses come to enrich themselves. It would be the final chance of the year, for the last fairs were past and there would be no more until spring.

They bought sausages and buns and fruit from various vendors and sat on the ground before the pavilion to lay in a hearty breakfast. There was hard fighting ahead, and they would need sustenance. Wulf made a small fire and heated watered and spiced wine to drive away the morning chill.

The greater lords and ladies were beginning to arrive from the city, where they had been guests at the palace or in the great houses. They were splendidly and colorfully dressed and were followed by trains of servants and armor bearers. Many were accompanied by musicians, and a few had dwarfs and other freakish attendants to amuse them.

After all were in their places, the king arrived. Naturally, his was the largest retinue. He had more monkeys than the others had servants. His huntsmen led dozens of hounds, as if this were a hunt rather than a tourney. His falconers carried priceless birds on their wrists. His dwarfs and jesters were even more grotesquely deformed than those of the nobles. His musicians played continuously and discordantly.

Falcon could not make out much of the king himself. He was too far away, and the king was so swathed in state robes that he might as well have been a mummer in a play. There was a lady at his side, but whether she was the queen or a mistress he could not determine.

The king took his place on the lavish dais set up for the royal household. The others found their seats, and servants provided them with wine and platters of comfits. When the king was satisfied that his party was settled in, he raised a hand and trumpeters sounded a fanfare. The crowd fell silent as a royal herald stepped to the edge of the dais.

"The royal tourney is now declared open," he called. "All knights and squires of good blood who wish to do battle for their honor and the honor of their ladies, come forward!"

Falcon, glittering in his newly burnished mail, his shield bright with fresh paint, rode forward with the mob of horsemen to halt before the dais. In the press of horses, Falcon could see little more of the monarch than he had seen before. He did see that there was a tall, saturnine man seated slightly behind and to the left of the king. This man wore the white robe and red cross of the Temple. To occupy such a place, he could only be the grand master of the order.

"My friends," the king said, "I know that you will strive with all your strength to prove your valor and your love for your ladies." He went on in this vein for some time, stressing the values of chivalry and the duty owed to his royal self to make this a memorable occasion. Falcon scanned the crowd on the dais in search of familiar faces. Yes, there was Gudrun. He wondered who was keeping her company of nights, and surveyed the crowd curiously. The king? No, he didn't have the haggard look of one who had spent the previous night in amorous contest with a Valkyrie. The royal address ended and the knights waved their lances and swords and cheered themselves silly. Then they rode back to their places, clearing the field.

The event was to open with a few grudge matches, some of them challenges dating back years. For most of its short history, the tourney had consisted entirely of the melee, in which two mounted forces collided as in war. Jousting, in which single combatants challenged each other, was relatively new. It was becoming enormously popular because it allowed the fighters to show off to best advantage for the admiration of the audience.

Falcon leaned on the wooden barrier that separated the knight's campground from the field. Hugh and Wulf leaned beside him. An immense crowd stretched as far as the eye could discern in every direction. All Paris was on holiday to see the royal tourney. The herald announced the first contestants. There was a rumble of hooves as the armored men charged down upon each other. Then there was a crash as lance met shield and the first loser of the tourney landed on his mailed back.

"Kept his point too low," Hugh said.

"No," Falcon protested, "he braced himself half a heartbeat too soon. That was why his point dropped."

"He was a fool to go out there in the first place," Wulf said.

"Shut up, Wulf," said Falson.

The next pair rode out, and another brief battle left one groaning on the ground. The third pair made a better show. Both lances were placed perfectly and snapped upon impact. The riders drew their swords and circled one another, hewing and guarding, until at length the stronger split his opponent's shield, breaking the arm behind it. The loser had no choice but to yield.

"Excellent!" Hugh said, grinning. "It's good to see two skillful men at play." Falcon nodded.

Soon the prearranged matches were over and the challenge fights began. Propped up on the railing where Hugh and Falcon leaned were the knight's shields. Any who had a mind to fight rode up to a shield and tapped it with his lance. The owner of the shield was obliged to answer the challenge. Young knights out to prove their mettle sought out famous champions. More experienced men looked for those who could put up a good fight but were not a match for themselves.

Hugh was challenged twice by young glory hunters. He defeated both neatly. Grinning all over his face, he returned to the barrier. Falcon was as yet unchallenged. "You're an unknown," Hugh explained. "They're buzzing with talk about you around here. Some think you're a famous champion in disguise.

Anyone can see you're an experienced man from the East, and that white blaze in your hair has the ladies talking. In any case, you have all your teeth, so you must know how to handle yourself."

Falcon smiled grimly. His helmet left most of his face bare. Only a man who was expert with his shield could keep all his teeth through a lifetime of training and warfare.

The next challenge proved to be the most interesting combat so far. Sir Rollo Dupré rode out. Slowly, he rode down the line of shields. Each time he stopped before one, Falcon could see the owner begin to sweat. Rollo drew rein before Falcon and stared at the device and at the tall knight with the white blaze for a long, tense moment. Falcon stared back as steadily. Rollo rode on down the barrier, and Hugh let out a long-pent breath. "Maybe you'll live to see nightfall after all." Falcon shrugged.

At last, Rollo tapped a shield. A young knight in exceptionally fine armor picked up the shield and mounted. Falcon could see that his face was ashen. He appeared to be no more than eighteen. Then his face was hidden behind his iron mask. The combatants cantered to opposite ends of the field. At a blast of the trumpets, they charged. They met in the center, almost directly in front of the king. The young knight went backward out of his saddle. Rollo rode around the downed man. The young knight struggled to his feet, his sword out.

"Stay down, you young fool!" Hugh shouted. He could not be heard above the roaring of the crowd. Without compunction, Sir Rollo took up his ax and rode the young knight down. The knight on the ground had time for one feeble blow, easily blocked, then the ax crunched into the mail covering his neck. He fell in an inert heap, his blood soaking into the earth. The crowd applauded gaily as Sir Rollo waved his bloody ax aloft.

"Well," said Hugh, "there's the first killing of the tourney. I'll wager it won't be the last."

Challenge followed challenge, and the ground became churned up by hooves. There were more fatalities, although none were as deliberate as that perpetrated by Rollo Dupré. Still Falcon received no challenges. He in turn challenged nobody. He would be just as happy not to take part in the jousting in any case. He planned to distinguish himself in the melee. That was the type of battlefield work he excelled at.

The day was most over, and Rollo wanted another match. Once again, the huge knight rode down the line of shields. Once again, he left a trail of sweating, relieved faces. Once again, he stopped before Falcon's shield. This time, he spoke.

"Your name, sir?" Rollo asked. His voice was oddly high-pitched for such a forbidding man.

"Sir Draco Falcon."

"I've never heard of you."

"I'm new here," Falcon said.

"Have you ever jousted in tourney before?" Rollo asked.

"Never," Falcon answered.

"Then let me have the honor of initiating you." Rollo tapped the falcon shield with his lance point. Then he rode to his end of the field.

"Now you're in for it." Hugh said. "Remember, if he unhorses you, don't get up."

"Kill him first chance you get, master," Wulf said. "Now that I think of it, let me go get your Saracen bow. If it looks like he's winning, I'll shoot him and you can get away while they're chasing me."

"I'm sorry, Wulf, but the king would never understand." Falcon mounted and pulled the mail coif over his head. He donned his helmet and tied its chin cord. Wulf handed him his shield, and he slipped his forearm through its straps, adjusting them until he was satisfied that it was secure. Then Wulf hung his ax from his saddlebow. Nemesis was too precious to risk in the tourney. In any case, she was an instrument for precision killing, and not suited to this kind of rough-and-tumble. He took his long lance and rode to the end of the field opposite Rollo.

There was a last-minute checking of equipment along with a good deal of speculation about the unknown knight who was almost certainly about to die. The ladies were wistful, because he looked so handsome and gallant. The younger knights and squires assumed he would not last long, because his equipment was antiquated and although he was a big man he seemed almost frail in comparison with the brutish Sir Rollo. But the more experienced knights held their counsel. They could see, merely by the way he sat his horse, that Sir Draco was going to be no easy conquest for Rollo Dupré.

The king watched the two knights in happy anticipation. He made a tiny signal with his hand, and the trumpets snarled. With a lurch, the two mounts thundered forward. Clods flew from beneath their hooves as the riders lowered lances and raised shields. Falcon kept his eyes on the lance point opposite. It was perfectly steady, as was his own. Rollo's shield rim was held just below the eye slots of his helm.

Falcon held his shield a bit lower, uncovering a hand's breadth of unprotected flesh beneath the rim of his helmet. At the last instant before collision, Rollo jerked his point up, straight for Falcon's eyes. Falcon had exposed the target to draw the lance, and he leaned slightly forward. The point whispered over his head, ticking slightly against the point of his helmet, just as his own point slammed into the upper edge of Rollo's shield, smashing it back against the iron covering his face.

Then they were past each other, Rollo reeling in his saddle and dropping his lance. Falcon turned and prepared for another charge. Without his lance, Rollo would have little chance, and that suited Falcon. Then he saw that his own lance was cracked for almost its whole length from the shattering force of the blow. He cursed and dropped the useless lance. Then the ax was in his hand, and he saw that Rollo had revived and had his own ax at the ready.

The crowd was cheering wildly. Even the least knowledgeable could see that Falcon had accomplished the neatest bit of lanceplay in the tourney so far. Aficionados were volubly discussing the fine points of what had just happened. Then the noise abated a bit as the next act approached.

Falcon and Rollo trotted slowly toward each other. There was no sense charging with axes. When they were five feet apart, Rollo dug in his spurs and his mount surged against Falcon's. The bigger horse almost bowled Falcon's mount over as Rollo's ax came down. Falcon jerked his shield up in time and just managed to stay in his saddle as his horse staggered beneath him. Rollo kept up his blows, not giving Falcon time to strike in return. Suddenly, Falcon's mount had had enough. It spun on its forehooves and kicked Rollo's horse in the side. The injured horse shrilled and bolted away. Rollo needed several seconds to regain control of the steed, which Falcon employed to catch his breath and calm his own destrier. The crowd was mad with excitement, cheering and clapping with the joy of mobs who get to see men in mortal danger without being at any risk themselves.

When the two closed for the second bout with

axes, Falcon struck as soon as Rollo was within range. He swung overhand, forcing the other man to keep raising his shield. Since the axhead formed an angle with its shaft, it could strike a blow several inches past the shield, even if the haft was blocked. Thus the shield had to be raised higher than it would against a sword cut from the same angle. Falcon kept the man blinded by his own shield, his arm growing tired from repeatedly lifting the heavy defense.

Rollo knew perfectly well what Falcon's strategy was, and he began throwing long, looping horizontal blows aimed at Falcon's side. Alarmed, Falcon drew back. There was a particularly deadly move used by expert axmen in which the attacker would rush in until he was shield to shield with his enemy. The instant the two shields touched, he would swing his ax in a wide, vicious horizontal arc around the other man's shield and body to bring the edge smashing into kidney or spine. The blow would lack the force to split the mail, but the pain would be sufficient to drop the victim, leaving him to be finished at leisure. Falcon was sure that Rollo was trying to force an opening for that blow.

The two horses drew apart for a few moments as the men sat gasping. The roaring from the crowd had become almost demented. Rollo spurred his horse into a short charge, swinging his ax at Falcon's arm, but he was tiring and the blow was not quite as swift as the earlier ones. Falcon jerked back the hand holding his shield's handle. The kite-shaped shield pivoted around his arm, and its long point cracked solidly into Rollo's elbow. Rollo rode past howling, his ax dangling by its wrist thong, his arm temporarily paralyzed. Falcon grinned as he wheeled his horse to follow. He was going to ax Rollo in the back before he had a chance to turn around.

Suddenly, men were rushing between the two, blocking Falcon's ax with long staves. What was this all about? "Oyez! Oyez!" shouted the chief herald. "The sun is now down and the combat is at an end! Let all lay down arms for the night!" With a flourish, the herald stepped back from the edge of the dais.

The king was clearly put out. "It's not sundown, is it?" he demanded.

"See, my liege: The sun has touched the horizon. By the rules of the herald's craft, that is the sign of dusk and the cessation of combat."

The king leaned forward as if a few more inches would give him a closer look at the sun. "It's not *quite* touching the horizon, I think. Surely there is time for a few more passes between these splendid knights."

"I am sorry, sire," the herald said, "but the rules are most specific."

"Oh, very well, then." He leaned back in his high chair and cast an eye over the mob, which was growing riotous in its disappointment. "We'll have to do something about *them*, though," he said, pointing at the crowd. "Hmm. You two!" He beckoned to Rollo and Falcon, who were sitting wearily on their weary horses. "Come here!" The two knights walked their horses to the royal dais.

"Splendidly fought, both of you," the king said. Seeing him closely for the first time, Falcon could tell that Philip Augustus was a man only four or five years older than himself, but the lines of care and responsibility made him look another ten years the elder. "You, Sir Rollo Dupré, and you, Sir, ah, Sir—" Gudrun leaned forward and whispered in the king's ear. "—Sir Draco Falcon, are a credit to knighthood, to manhood, and to the chivalry of France. The rules of heraldry have required that we halt this combat and declare a draw. Even so, we would see you strive again. On the day following tomorrow, weather permitting, we shall hold the grand melee. Sir Rollo, you shall command the red team. Sir Draco, you have charge of the white."

"Your highness does me too much honor," Rollo said.

"Possibly. But if I don't do something we'll have a riot on our hands." Falcon could not suppress a grin. The heralds were announcing the royal decision, and the growls changed to cheers at the prospect of an even bigger, deadlier fight between the two champions. With alarm, Falcon saw that Gudrun was watching him with an unmistakable gleam in her eye. Her ministrations were the last thing his aching body needed.

Falcon rode back to his tent, to be greeted by cheering knights as the champion of the day, although the match had been declared a draw. Hugh clapped him on the shoulder as he descended from his horse, and Wulf wore a look of the profoundest relief. "Why didn't you kill him?" the Saxon demanded. "You didn't have to let a few staves stop you."

"Not in front of the king, Wulf," Falcon said wearily. He didn't even feel up to arguing with Wulf.

"Hmpf," Wulf snorted. "So he'd've outlawed you. You've been outlawed before."

"Oh, silence, boy," Hugh said impatiently. "Your master's gaining a reputation he couldn't get in a hundred battles. Draco Falcon the soldier could spend a lifetime making his name. But Draco Falcon champion of the royal tourney, holder of King Philip's favor, that's something else. If he comes through the melee as well as he did today, nobles all over France will be clamoring for his services." Wulf had no answer to that, and he lapsed into a sulky silence.

"Wulf, go take care of my horse," Falcon ordered.

He and Hugh went to their shared tent, where Hugh helped him to disarm. Falcon bent forward as Hugh tugged at the hem of his mail, pulling it over his head and turning it inside out. As Falcon bent double, the heavy garment fell off of its own weight. He straightened, sighing with relief. He always felt as if he could fly, after disarming.

Hugh handed him a skin of wine, and he drank thirstily. Fighting gave a man a raging thirst. Then he remembered something. "Hugh, if an enormous German lady comes looking for me, you haven't seen me."

"Of course," Hugh said. "Need all your strength for the melee, eh?"

"She's a stouter opponent than Rollo Dupré," Falcon said.

From time to time that evening, knights came to the tent to congratulate Falcon and express their admiration for his excellent fighting that day. Many volunteered to ride at his side on the white team.

"Hugh," Falcon asked, "how are these teams arranged, and how do I go about leading mine?"

"The fighters are split into two roughly equal sides. One side wear white scarfs around their helms or their sword arms, and the other wear red. Two champions are chosen as leaders. On the day of the melee, the teams will be marshaled at opposite ends of the field, each behind a rope barrier stretched the width of the ground. When the trumpets blow, the heralds cut the ropes and the knights charge. Then they fight until all of one side are captured or dead, or until sundown."

"Of what does my leadership consist?"

"It is purely an honor," Hugh answered. "Each man fights for himself, to take as many prisoners for ransom as he can. The liveliest action is always in the center, and you can usually get some rest by riding to the outskirts of the fight. Sometimes, though, when spirits are high, the fighting will spill off the field and men will chase each other for miles."

Falcon strolled about the campground for a while, and he was frequently invited into a tent or to a gathering around a fire for wine and some food. He was not sure whether this was because he was suddenly popular or because Sir Rollo was so violently hated. He noticed that it was mainly the young and inexperienced knights who were so eager to join his side in the melee. The older men were unstinting in their praise but were not so anxious to take Falcon's side. He asked Hugh about this.

"They're playing safe," Hugh answered. "Nobody likes Rollo, but there's no denying he's a great champion."

"I would've had him today but for those heralds," Falcon said.

"Some see that as a fluke. In any case, in the melee, Rollo will have his men with him. They've worked together in a hundred tourneys and they know their business. For all these men's admiration of your fighting today, not one in three expects to see you alive after the melee."

This was a sobering speech. He had forgotten about those men of Rollo's. As he recalled, there were six of them, hard-bitten veterans by their look. He had taken on that many before and lived, but if they were a well-drilled team, they would have no difficulty in handling Draco Falcon. The greatest fighter in the world was only an individual, and a team who knew their tactics well could down the mightiest champion who ever lived.

The next day, the knights who had taken part in the jousting had an opportunity to rest while other festivities took place. There was a storming of the

Castle of Love, which Falcon avoided for the good of his digestion. Several times, Gudrun came looking for him, but Wulf or Hugh would misdirect her, to Falcon's great relief.

In the afternoon, sides were chosen for the next day's melee. Falcon sat his horse at one end of the field, Rollo at the other. All volunteers who wished to take one side or the other were asked to join their chosen leaders. As Falcon had expected, the bulk of the more experienced men chose Rollo. Many of those who held back also chose Rollo when they saw which way the wind was blowing. The remainder were divided roughly by the heralds until both sides were somewhat equal in number, although nobody thought to take a count.

The colored scarves were passed out to the riders, and Falcon looked over his men. They were young, for the most part, although he could see a few veterans who were taking sides with him for the sake of the richer ransoms to be had from the other team. Hugh, in a commendable display of loyalty, stood by him.

Then he spotted a face he had not expected to see. He guided his horse through the press until he was even with the other. "Claude de Coucy," Falcon said. "What are you doing here? Templars aren't allowed to take part in tourneys."

"I know," Claude said. "I have not yet taken my final vows."

"Do you intend to do so?"

"I think not," Claude said.

"Isabeau?" Falcon queried, cocking a white-tufted eyebrow.

"Yes," Claude said. "Sir Draco, until you took me to her that night, I had not realized how much I love her. I would die for her. I would—"

"Fight for her honor in a tourney?"

"Exactly. We watched the jousting yesterday. We were both thrilled by your fight with the vicious Rollo Dupré. I swore that I would fight by your side in the melee. Tomorrow, I shall wear her favor into battle."

Falcon grunted. Damned young fool. Well, death or maiming in a tourney was better than life in the Temple, as far as he was concerned. At least the girl was young enough to find herself another husband, should the worst happen. Those who wished to die of old age had no business in the knight's profession.

"I'm proud to have you among my men," Falcon said. Claude beamed joyfully.

After the choosing of sides, Falcon had his shield, badly battered by Rollo's ax, re-covered with leather and freshly painted. That evening, there was a minor banquet held on long tables near the pavilion. The greater banquet would be held in the palace after the melee. Falcon ate and drank moderately, for a hangover on the morrow could prove disastrous. For the same reason, he faded from view anytime he saw Gudrun.

EIGHT

THE MORROW proved to be another fine day for fighting. The sun shone bright, and the field had been oriented so that the sunrise was to the left or right as the knights faced their enemies, in order that neither side had the disadvantage of the sun in their eyes for the first charge.

According to the protocol of the heralds, Falcon and Rollo rode onto the field first, to stand before the king and his retinue. There were new murmurs today at Falcon's appearance, for now he was wearing his splendid Saracen mail and his long, curved sword, Nemesis. He had decided that he would only leave this field victorious or dead, so there was no sense fighting under the handicap of excessively heavy armor. He bore ax, lance, and dagger as well and in all cut a fine if somewhat exotic figure.

"Brave and valiant knights," the king began, "this is the crowning day of the tourney. To the victor of this day's combat will go all honor, and he will choose the Queen of Love and Beauty." Falcon saw Gudrun glowering at him. Woe to him if he chose any other.

"Sire?" This was from the grand master of the Temple.

"Yes?" Philip said.

"Your pardon, sire, but I am informed that there is one among Sir Draco's men who should not be permitted here."

"Is that so?" the king said. He turned to the royal herald. "Did you let in a degraded knight?"

"All have been most closely checked, sire," the herald answered.

"Not a degraded knight," the grand master said, "but a member of the Temple. You know that members of my order are forbidden to take part in tourneys."

"Is this true, Sir Draco?" queried the king.

"It is not, sire. There is one Sir Claude de Coucy among us. He was pledged to the Temple, but he has not taken his final vows and may do as he pleases."

"But he was to take his vows this very day!" said the grand master.

"Sorry," Philip said. "No final vows, no Templar." The grand master sat back frowning as the king turned back to the two knights. "I know that you will strive with all your might to make this a memorable occasion. I only ask that you give quarter when it is asked, and obey the instructions of the heralds. And now, the Archbishop of Paris wishes to speak."

A tall, gaunt man in severe garments rose and intoned the papal denunciation against tourneys. He informed the participants that any of them who died in such events were to be buried unshriven and without the last rites. They had all heard it before and paid not the slightest attention. In any case, the king was excommunicate and the country under interdict, so there could be no sacraments anyway. The knights did not like the idea of eternal damnation, but their class existed solely for the purpose of warfare and strife. If it came to a choice between fighting and salvation, they would choose fighting every time.

At the best of times the church was held in low esteem, or at least its minions were. The cult of chivalry had become almost a religion in itself, and the knights suspected, despite the words of the churchmen, that as long as they behaved honorably as knights should, they would be able to square things with God come Judgment Day.

Before they rode off to their separate ends of the field, Rollo gave Falcon a mad, malevolent grin so full of blood-lusting anticipation that even Falcon, hardened warrior that he was, felt a tingle of apprehension.

The knights were gathered at their respective ends of the field, and heralds were forcing them yet farther back, with their staves held horizontally. It was not an easy task, as every knight was intent upon being in the front line, where all the honor was. Falcon lowered his aventail and tilted his helmet back on his head.

"Get back behind the rope line or we'll never get started!" The whipcrack of his voice startled the knights into a general movement backward. Most of them had not been accustomed to such commands since their days as squires. "There'll be plenty of honor for everybody before this day's over. I want only knights of more than five years' experience in the front line. Those who have been on Crusade or have fought in battle for their lords or who have been in more than five tourneys, I want in the center near me."

Slowly, the knights sorted themselves out, and Falcon took his place in the center of the front line with Hugh on his right. The heralds were finally succeeding in getting their rope barrier stretched from fence to fence. Falcon took some satisfaction in seeing that Rollo was having much more difficulty in getting his men arranged. He glanced to the side and saw that Wulf was standing with a small group of men-at-arms, without weapons but helmeted and armored. These men had been hired to help Wulf extract Falcon from the fray should he be downed. Also, they would go in to fetch out any man who yielded to Falcon. It was risky work, and they demanded and got high pay.

At last, all was ready. The pennons of the knights fluttered and snapped in the brisk breeze. The horses stomped restlessly. Most of the knights wore brightly colored surcoats over their mail. The majority wore the face-covering helms that were now the fashion, and many of these were painted. Here and there could be seen knights who, like Falcon, preferred to keep their vision and hearing and wore round or conical helmets with a nasal bar to protect the nose. Mail and lance points glittered in the sun. Everywhere there was color and music and gaiety. It was, Falcon thought, a decidedly odd atmosphere to precede what was bound to be a sizable slaughter.

The trumpets blared, and men with axes cut the ropes. The two lines surged forward, and the cheers of the crowd blended with the war cries of the knights into a single, delirious sound of frenzy and excitement.

Over his shield, Falcon saw Rollo and his men charging straight for him in a compact mass, shaped like a wedge with Rollo as its tip. Falcon had no chance whatever with such a formation. As the two teams neared, the packed groups of knights opened somewhat and gave those in front a little leeway. Just before the moment of collision, Falcon swerved sharply to the left and Hugh to the right. They had planned this move the day before. They disrupted the charges of the flanking knights, but this was for their lives. Rollo and his knot of men burst between them and into the dismayed knights of Falcon's second line.

Falcon spotted a red-scarf knight before him and aimed his lance at the center of the man's shield. Taken at an awkward angle, the knight tumbled from his saddle. Foolishly, the man tried to struggle to his feet, and Falcon conked him soundly on the back of the helm with the blunt side of his ax.

The ground was now littered with dropped lances and fallen men as the hand-to-hand battle began. Two red-scarf knights teamed up for an attack on Falcon, one coming from each side. Falcon ducked beneath the sword of the one on his right and gave him a backhand blow to the kidney as he rode past. The second, on the left, he dealt with by blocking the sword with his shield, then bringing his shield rim up beneath the man's chin, behind the iron mask. He spurred his horse to get away from the press, not waiting to see whether the two were unhorsed. An enemy knight loomed up before him, and the two men dealt one another simultaneous overhand strokes. Both blocked and neither scored. Then they were forced apart by more battling knights. Falcon spotted a relatively clear area and rode to it. He spun his horse in a tight circle to scan the scene and make sure nobody was coming up behind him.

The melee was a spectacle of utter confusion as men wheeled and hacked at one another with no semblance of order. Underfoot, servants were hauling out their masters' trophies at risk to their lives. Some of the knights carried bags of gold, so that they could pay their ransoms and be back in the fight without wasting time. Here and there, footmen serving different lords were breaking into fights over possession of particularly lucrative captives.

A knight who had fetched a fresh lance couched it and charged Falcon. Falcon sat his horse calmly, facing the knight, his shield held low. When the lance point was no more than three feet away, Falcon moved. With his ax, he parried the lance upward, continuing the motion until the weapon was overhead, then bringing it down with a crash on the opposite helm. The knight fell like a sandbag. Falcon saw that the helm was not split, only dented. The blow had been seen by the crowd, who cheered its exquisite timing.

Two more men rode up, and Falcon readied himself, but then he saw the white kerchiefs and identified the shields as belonging to Hugh and Claude. The two pulled off their helms as they reined in beside him.

"How many have you taken, Draco?" asked Hugh.

"I've engaged five. Downed two of 'em for sure, and another two possibles. The other I didn't touch."

"I've got one," Hugh said.

"How have you fared, Claude?" Falcon asked.

"I've fought two. They're still mounted, but then, so am I."

"Well, this thing's just started," Falcon said. "Where's Rollo?"

Hugh pointed to a group of a dozen men sitting on the sidelines whom nobody seemed inclined to challenge. "Over there, waiting for men to tire, as usual."

"Well," Falcon said. "Let's not follow their example. Come on!" As his companions rehelmed, Falcon saw Wulf and his men coming to take the man he'd knocked unconscious. The three knights rode into the thick of the fighting, with Falcon in the center, the other two slightly behind him and to either side. They bulled their way through, slashing efficiently whenever they encountered a red scarf. Then they were through and out the other side, almost directly below the king on his dais.

"Bravely fought, Sir Draco!" called Philip. "And you others, too!" The king looked beyond them. " 'Ware Sir Rollo, now, my lads!"

Falcon turned to see Rollo and his men charging down upon them. They all had lances. There was only one reasonably safe place. "Back into the melee," he shouted, loud enough for his companions to hear him through their helms. They spurred back into the fight, where there was danger on all sides, but it was not as concentrated as that posed by Sir Rollo and his killers.

Falcon rode about like a madman, whirling his ax and shouting: "To me! To me! Whites rally to me!" Here and there, white-scarf knights heard and rode over to Falcon. In the same fashion, Rollo was gathering a larger collection of the red knights. The white force was now decidedly smaller, having lost more men through capture. They were being hemmed in against the wooden barrier by the red force, and for a few minutes the fighting became desultory as the two forces sought to rearrange themselves. Then the reds turned and rode back half the width of the field. The whites stared at them in mystification. Clearly, this was something prearranged. Then the reds wheeled and faced the whites in a massive wedge.

"They're going to charge!" someone shouted.

"Scatter!" Falcon yelled. With their backs to the barrier, they would have to take the full, murderous force of the charge, the weight of at least two hundred horses, riders, and armor. Some of the whites at the outer edges of the outnumbered force managed to get clear, but it was too late for the greater part of them.

The red force smashed into the whites with the power of an avalanche overwhelming an Alpine village. The whites were slammed back against the wooden barrier. Falcon's horse was forced back by the weight of the other mounts, scrambling desperately to keep its footing while Falcon strove frantically to protect himself with his shield.

Then, with a rending crunch, the barrier was down and the horsemen were spilling out onto the common ground, the citizenry screaming and fleeing in panic. The crowd of spectators was dense, and many were trampled. Some knights callously cut down townsmen to clear their path. Those spectators who were not in immediate danger cheered at this new sport.

"To the village! Whites, to the village!" Falcon screamed. With a small force, he galloped toward the huddle of buildings nearby. The few villagers still there boggled in disbelief to see the mass of bloody, filthy knights bearing down on their little town like some nightmarish vision out of Revelation. They dashed for doorways and bolted the doors from inside, then their heads appeared in the upper windows, ready to watch the fun.

The whites stormed into the narrow street of the village, scattering chickens, pigs, ducks, goats, dogs, and other livestock. With the tourney nearby, the street was full of vendors' stalls, booths selling produce, and all the trappings of a market day. These were quickly reduced to splinters and horses slid in the squashed fruit and churned up mud produced by the smashed casks of wine.

Falcon rallied the men to produce some sort of

united front across the narrow street, where the reds could not take advantage of their superior numbers. Then the reds were there. Fortunately, by this time their horses were too tired to charge with full force. Falcon blocked a mace and crushed the wielder's shoulder with his ax. Then he was being forced inexorably back by the weight of the opposing force. A low-hanging inn sign smashed him on the back of his head, half stunning him, then a sword stroke, imperfectly blocked, toppled him from his saddle. Falcon crashed against the inn door, smashing it inward and tumbling inside onto the straw-covered floor. A gaggle of geese flapped and honked away from him. As he scrambled to his feet, Falcon saw that the place was full of animals and poultry, doubtless shooed inside out of harm's way by the innkeeper.

The doorway was now blocked by the inert carcasses of a horse and several men. Falcon spotted a stairway and made for it, having to deal along the way with the charge of an enraged gander. He kicked a pig off the stair and made his way to an upper room, the door of which he unceremoniously kicked open.

He heard a shriek, and saw a woman turn from a window, snatching up a shift to cover her naked, plump, white body. The small shift was entirely inadequate for the task, but Falcon was paying little attention. He rushed at the window. The woman thought he was lunging at her, and with a little squeal she jumped aside, but not very far. Ignoring her, Falcon thrust open the windowpanes and looked down into the street. All was chaos below, red and white snarled in an inextricable mass.

"Ah, sir knight," the woman said, "please do not think me immodest. I was bathing when the fighting reached the street below. I could not resist a look, even in my state of undress."

"Think nothing of it," Falcon demurred. "I was the one who kicked the door in." Then he thought of something. "Did you say bath?" He looked around and saw a big tub of steaming water.

"Yes," the woman said, her gaze going to the tub. "Would you care to join me?"

"Thank you, you are most kind, but I really haven't the time." Falcon strode to the tub, unlacing his helm and throwing back his coif. He dropped to his knees and plunged his head into the water. Although it was steaming, to his overheated flesh it felt deliciously cool and refreshing. He withdrew his head and shook it like a wet dog. "Towel?" he asked.

The woman handed him the shift with which she had been covering herself. He dried himself vigorously. "Could I trouble you for something to drink, lady?" Falcon asked courteously.

"But of course," she said. Her breasts bobbled fetchingly as she crossed the small room to a chest upon which stood a pitcher and cup. She poured a cup and took cup and pitcher to Falcon. She handed him the pitcher and drank from the cup herself.

Falcon sluiced his parched throat with the soothing wine. He set the pitcher down. "Thank you, lady," he said. "You are most hospitable, considering the circumstances."

She blushed prettily. "It's the least I can do for a gallant knight who is fighting for his very life." She leaned out the window and looked at the bloody chaos below. "I think, sir, that they will be fighting for some time longer. Will you not relax here with me? You can always join them later." She sat on the bed and patted the space beside her. It was sorely tempting. Then he looked outside. It was clearing a little. He turned to the woman.

"I fear not. I must rejoin my men."

"After the fight, then?"

"If I am still alive, count on it." She smiled. He was about to rehelm when he remembered his manners. He crossed to the bed and lifted the woman from it bodily. With one big hand about her waist and the other beneath her slightly damp buttocks, he kissed her fiercely. She sighed and thrust her tongue into his mouth. She tasted faintly of cloves.

Falcon dropped the woman back upon the bed and returned to the window, raising his coif and putting his helmet on. She waved at his disappearing back as he leaped from the window.

Falcon descended upon a knight with a red scarf. He got an arm around the man's neck and yanked him to the ground, pulling the man's helm off in the process. As the red knight struggled to his feet, Falcon smashed him in the face with his spiked gauntlet. He mounted the downed knight's horse and looked around. For the moment, the street was almost clear. He looked up to see the woman, whose name he had forgotten to ask, leaning out the window and smiling. He blew her a kiss and rode off in search of the fighting.

Near the edge of the village he found Wulf and the hired men, accompanied by a small band of knights he did not recognize. Then he realized that these must be the ones he had defeated. He had not thought there were so many. Wulf spotted him and trotted over. He held Falcon's shield.

"I found this in the village street, my lord." Wulf said, handing it up.

"I lost my ax someplace," Falcon said. "No matter. Where's the fighting?"

"Most of the knights have made their way back to the tourney field. Why don't you just sit the rest of it out?"

"Where are Hugh and Claude?" Wulf shrugged. "Is Rollo still active?" Falcon asked.

"The last I saw of him, he was," Wulf answered.

"I'm back for the tourney, then," Falcon said. He turned his horse and trotted easily back to the tourney ground. He could see that the fighting was raging among the tents now, and most of them were down. Men and horses were falling, feet and hooves entangled in the tent ropes.

Falcon skirted the edge of the campground and found Hugh and Claude, miraculously still mounted, taking a breather with their helmets off near the great hole smashed in the wooden barrier. Falcon rode up to them, carefully avoiding trampling the bodies of knights and townsmen that lay all around.

Claude saw him first. "Sir Draco!" he said, smiling broadly. "We thought we'd lost you back there. Where have you been?"

"Oh," Falcon replied. "I found a lady with a bath and thought I'd rest awhile." The other two laughed uproariously. "Now, Falcon said, "where's Rollo?"

Hugh pointed toward the royal dais. "There's the damned bugger," he said. "He's been sitting on his ass for the last half hour or more. Once in a while, he sends one of his men to pick up someone who's staggering. Damned coward!"

Falcon could see that King Philip was standing at the edge of the dais, haranguing Rollo, obviously urging him to reenter the fray. Rollo was just as clearly having none of it. Falcon looked at his companions. Neither seemed wounded, and both of their horses looked to be in good condition. Falcon pointed at Rollo.

"That bastard's lived long enough," Falcon said. "Are you with me?"

Hugh and Claude looked at the men before the dais.

Rollo had four of his band remaining. "Five to three," he mused. Then he grinned from ear to ear. "Sure, why not?"

Falcon looked at Claude. The boy was a little pale, but he nodded. Falcon got some boys who were busy robbing the bodies to scavenge them three sound lances.

"Let's go!" Falcon said, setting in his spurs. The three steeds leaped forward as one.

At the royal dais, Philip was berating Rollo. "Sir Rollo Dupré," he shouted, "you are a false and recreant knight and a disgrace to chivalry! I can have you struck from the rolls for this cowardice!" Rollo was bearing the harangue with stoic calm. Then a babble of voices from behind him made Philip look up. His bearded royal jaw dropped in awe. From the other side of the field, three knights with white scarves were charging the royal dais, full tilt.

"Best look to yourself, Sir Rollo!" the king said. "It seems the fight is coming to you."

Cursing, Rollo and his men tried to wheel their mounts to meet this new onslaught, but it was clear that they were far too late. To everyone's amazement, the three attackers did not even attempt to slow their mounts; they intended to collide with knights and dais at full speed.

"Madmen!" the grand master said.

"Yes, it's that Draco Falcon fellow," the king said delightedly. "He must be truly insane, but what style!"

Hugh reached his chosen target first. His lance took his man's shield so perfectly and with such power that it pierced the shield and passed through the man's breast and out his back with an audible snapping of mail links, nailing him securely to the front of the dais. The force of the collision knocked Hugh back over his cantle and onto the ground.

Claude struck next. His lance touched his opponent's shield slightly off center, but still with enough force to send the man slamming back into the dais. The force of his horse colliding with the other mount sent Claude flying over both steeds to crash to the ground beyond.

Falcon struck last. Rollo had just had time to brace himself and get shield and lance into position. Both lance points touched the shields opposite at the same instant. The force was so tremendous that both horses were forced up to their hind legs as the lances bent like two full-drawn bows. For an instant, the action seemed to freeze into unbearable tension as men, horses, and lances absorbed the full power of the terrible charge. Then the lances parted with a snap so loud that it turned heads for the full extent of the battleground.

Both horses came down, and Falcon dropped the stump of his lance as one of Rollo's men attacked his unshielded side with his sword. Falcon released his shield and grasped the sheath of Nemesis with his left hand as he seized her grip in his right. For one second, he seemed to have no defense against the sword, then Nemesis was out in a flash too swift to be seen and he cut the attacker's hand off at the wrist between mail sleeve and armored glove. Hand and sword went flying and the maimed knight screamed.

At the same instant, Rollo struck Falcon's mount between the eyes with his ax. As the horse fell, Falcon jumped clear, now gripping Nemesis in both fists. With a quick, economical cut, he slashed Rollo's reins. robbing him of control of his mount. With a dextrous kick, Falcon booted the horse in the nose. It reared indignantly, casting its rider to the ground.

Rollo's remaining horseman made to charge down on Falcon, but Hugh leaped up and dragged him from the saddle. As the man fell to the ground, Claude wrestled his helm off and Hugh stood and made a short hop into the air, coming down with both feet in the man's face.

Rollo Dupré scrambled to his feet and roared an obscenity as he dragged out his sword. To Falcon, it seemed that the man was moving with incredible slowness. It was almost like one of the pantomime exercises he had practiced with Suleiman. Falcon stepped forward, Nemesis held low and to one side. He carefully stepped into a puddle of blood and pretended to slip. He went down on one knee, lowering the curved sword still farther, turning it so that the razor edge was upward.

Rollo let out a bellow of triumph as he lumbered forward, his sword held in both hands and raised behind his right shoulder for the kill. He stood straddle-legged, and now Falcon had the opportunity and all the time he needed. Just bring Nemesis up between the brute's widespread legs and split him beneath the hauberk from crotch to navel.

Suddenly, blood sprang from Rollo's eyeslits. The man stood for a moment, then toppled like a tree. Falcon had to scramble out of the way. Behind Rollo stood Claude de Coucy, and buried in the back of Rollo's helm was Claude's ax. The people on the dais and all around were cheering madly. Falcon was unimpressed. They would have cheered as loudly had he been the one killed. He staggered to his feet and crossed to stand before the dais. There he stood back to back with Claude and Hugh to await the rest of the red force. Knights began to gather, and Falcon scanned them, but all seemed to be wearing white scarves.

"Sire," said the herald, "it seems that the white side is victorious." At this, the assembled whites let forth a hoarse, ragged cheer. Falcon made a rough count. About a hundred seemed to be still on their feet.

"Sir Draco," said King Philip, "I declare you champion of the tourney. It is now your privilege to name the Queen of Love and Beauty."

Falcon saw Gudrun looking at him hungrily. He gazed out over the churned, bloody field, the destroyed camp, the wrecked village. He turned back to the king. "Sire, I fear I must decline this honor."

"Decline? Why?"

"Because, at the last, I was defeated. Sir Rollo Dupré would have slain me, had it not been for my friend Sir Claude de Coucy. It was he who slew Sir Rollo, and I say that Sir Claude should be champion."

The king seemed nonplussed, but then he caught the frown on the face of the grand master, and he smiled, seeing an opportunity to discomfit his enemy. "Very well. This is a most chivalrous concession, Sir Draco. I hereby declare Sir Claude de Coucy to be the champion of the royal tourney!"

There arose a great cheer, and helpful shoulders hoisted Claude into his saddle. A lance was handed up to him, and he lowered its point toward the lady who sat next to Philip. She was, in fact, the most recent queen, Agnes of Meran. She picked up a chaplet exquisitely fashioned in the form of a laurel wreath from thin gold sheet and draped it on the end of the lance.

Carefully, Claude rode the length of the dais. Near the end, where members of the visiting minor nobility were seated, he extended it to Isabeau de Clare. The diminutive lady took it and set it upon her brow, blushing furiously all the while. A court noble came and escorted her to the royal dais, where King Philip took her hand and kissed her on both cheeks. He then turned to the assembled knights. Many more, wearing both colors, had come staggering and limping in.

"All of you who can still walk or be carried are invited to a grand banquet to be held at the palace this evening. I now declare the royal tourney to be closed."

There was a final, feeble cheer, and the knights turned to go in search of their destroyed tents and belongings. "Is that all?" Falcon asked Hugh.

"That's it," the knight answered. "Let's go collect our ransoms and find a place to get drunk before the banquet."

They found Wulf guarding the captives, and terms were quickly agreed upon. Wulf had also located Falcon's horse. As soon as he was disarmed, Falcon mounted.

"Where are you going?" asked Hugh.

"As a knight, I have certain obligations," Falcon answered. "I'll see you at the banquet tonight." He left them looking mystified. As he rode for the village, he wondered if the bath water was still warm.

NINE

THE KING'S palace was a new sort of building. It was strong, but not fortified as would be a castle. The walls were not so thick that the interior was cramped. There were a great many rooms, allowing the residents a measure of privacy. Falcon couldn't decide quite what to call it, but it reminded him of some of the fine mansions he'd seen in the Holy Land.

The huge space of the great hall was thronged with guests and servants when he arrived. The hall was one of the largest he'd ever seen, easily a hundred paces long and thirty wide. This vast open space was made possible by the relatively thin walls and the roof overhead, which was made of wood, so ingeniously pieced together that no internal supports were necessary.

A big silver goblet of wine was thrust into Falcon's hand as soon as he entered the hall. Torches and candles burned everywhere, and the straw that crunched underfoot was fresh and fragrant. A courtier saw Falcon studying the intricate carpentry of the ceiling and joined him.

"The king knighted the master carpenter for that," the courtier announced. "You are Draco Falcon, hero of the tourney, are you not?"

"I'm Falcon, but you're thinking of Claude de Coucy."

The courtier laughed. "Young de Coucy was named the champion, but everyone knows that you were the hero. I am Peter de Maine, a *bailli* of the royal lands near Meaux." This, then, was one of the class of seneschals who administered the royal estates, as powerful as any baron but answerable only to the king.

"When will Philip be joining us?" Falcon asked.

"When it pleases him, I suppose," Peter answered. "He spends much time with his mistresses and his hawks and attending to business."

"What business occupies the king these days?" Falcon asked blandly.

"What does not?" Peter said. "He has an empire to retake from the English, and certain—ah—understandings to arrive at with the Holy Father"—by this he meant the hard-fought curbings of church power in France—"and certain fractious barons to subdue; and—oh, the list is endless."

"A daunting prospect," Falcon said, "even without one too many wives and an excommunication and papal ban."

"Umm, yes, there's that, too. An unwise move, putting away Ingeborg, and I told him so myself. Wise as he is, I fear that our sovereign is no wiser than other men where women are concerned."

Falcon scanned the other guests. He spotted none

that he knew. Everywhere, little groups of tumblers and musicians were entertaining the guests. Dancing bears capered and huge dogs chased one another and wrestled with dwarfs. The light from the torches flickered over immense tapestries, still so bright and unstained by smoke that they must have been woven especially for this new palace.

Peter de Maine wandered away, and Falcon circulated himself among the guests, wondering when the banquet was to begin. He was ravenously hungry. The strenuous tourney and the more pleasant but equally demanding activities which followed had given an acute edge to his usually more than hearty appetite.

Soon he was relieved to see the servants setting up trestles. These were wooden framework supports of the kind used by carpenters to hold wood for sawing. When the trestles were set up, long boards were laid upon them to form tables, and the boards were covered with fine linen. The trestle tables were arranged so that there were two enormously long tables running the full length of the hall. At one end, there was a raised dais upon which stood a table that spanned the width of the hall at right angles to the two long tables. The high table was for the king and his most honored guests.

Benches were arranged on the outer sides of the tables, leaving the center space open for the servants to bring in and serve the platters of food. Salt cellars were laid out lavishly, bringing murmurs of admiration at the spendthrift extravagance of so much salt at a single banquet. Falcon tried to calculate how much the salt and the precious vessels might be worth. It boggled the mind.

It came to him that this was what the tourney had

been all about in the first place. A few years ago, Philip had been little more than a beggar king, surrounded by powerful enemies, betrayed by disloyal barons, his inheritance almost entirely frittered away by his pious but foolish father, his kingdom little more than an island.

Tonight, nobles and royal representatives from much of Europe were here to see his brilliant new palace, his lavish hospitality, his splendid tourney and banquet. Philip Augustus was announcing himself as a monarch to be reckoned with. Falcon didn't doubt that there was more than a bit of mummery to all this, and he wondered whether Philip had gone even further into debt to finance this show. Then he remembered the grand master.

Had Philip indebted himself to the Templars? If so, why would they kill him before they were paid back? Or were they afraid that he would attack the Temple to cancel his debt? Falcon was suddenly overwhelmed by his inexperience at power politics as it was played on an international scale. Then he remembered that there was somebody here who might be able to help him if properly approached.

He found Fra Benedetto chatting urbanely with a small group of noblemen and their ladies. They made way for him, instantly recognizing Falcon as the man who had made the tourney so memorable.

"Ah, Sir Draco," said Benedetto. "Welcome. I am informed that you distinguished yourself admirably in that barbarous event this afternoon. My congratulations." Falcon accepted the backhanded compliment with good grace.

"You know Sir Draco?" said one of the ladies. She gave Falcon the kind of appraising look that he was beginning to get used to here.

"We traveled here in company," Benedetto said.

"Sir Draco preserved us from some most unpleasant people."

"Sir Draco," said one of the men, "I understand that you are some kind of free captain, with your own private army, is this so?"

"Yes, that's true," Falcon answered.

"Before you leave Paris, I would like a few words with you, if you please." The man was dressed richly enough to be a major baron. Hugh had been right.

"It will be my honor," Falcon answered. He turned to Benedetto. "Holy father," he began, and Benedetto's eyebrow raised a fraction at this sudden respect, "there are certain matters which you might, of your goodness, be able to advise me about, if you would."

"For the good of your soul, no doubt," the churchman said, the corner of his mouth quirking slightly upward.

"Most decidedly," Falcon confirmed. The others present smiled, gratified to see that the strange knight was devout as well as chivalrous.

"I shall, of course, be most happy to provide counsel."

"I am most grateful," Falcon replied. There was a blast of trumpets, and all eyes turned to the end of the hall which held the high table. Through a curtain hanging at that end strode the king, and on his arm was the queen. He bowed slightly toward the guests, and there was much bowing in return. The king took his seat, and the guests went in search of their own.

Falcon wasn't sure where he was supposed to sit. He was not familiar with royal protocol and knew that he would be doing himself a disservice if he sat below the place dictated by his station. Then he spotted Hugh and decided that it would be safe to sit near him. Hugh beamed and made space for Draco next to him.

"I could eat a bear, Draco, how about you?" Hugh had already shipped a good deal of wine.

"The same," Falcon answered.

The first courses began to arrive. On enormous salvers, servitors carried in whole roast boars, deer with their heads replaced and their antlers gilded, peacocks roasted and their feathers carefully replaced, roast bear in a piquant sauce, long spits each skewering five or six fowl stuffed with walnuts, platters of eels, huge fish baked whole, pastries full of mussels and oysters. The fare seemed to have no end.

Guests reached out and grabbed whatever took their fancy, as other servants passed out bread trenchers—wide platters of flat, hard-baked bread with a raised rim to hold in the meat juices. These served the guests as plates. Falcon carved slabs of meat with his dagger as the platters passed, and speared fish and eels onto his trencher with the skill of long practice. As a young squire at Odo FitzRoy's castle in Normandy, he had had to fight with the other squires for every mouthful. Nor had he been averse to breaking a few bones to get an especially succulent morsel.

"If we'd had to wait much longer," Hugh said, loosening his belt, "I'd've fought my way through the palace guard to get to the kitchen." He took a generous pinch of salt from the nearest cellar and scattered it over the heap of flesh on his trencher. Cheeses, and rolls made of fine white flour, were being distributed, and serving girls and pages dashed about with pitchers of wine to keep the guests' cups filled.

It looked extravagant and wasteful, but Falcon knew that it was not. What the guests left on the tables, the servants would fall upon like a plague of locusts. The scraps, bones, and gravy-soaked trenchers would then be distributed among the beggars who flocked outside. The rigors of winter were ahead, and the livestock and game had to be thinned, for there was never enough feed to keep all alive through winter. Little of the meat, fish, and produce could be preserved through the long months ahead, so it was better to consume it in a few great feasts than let it spoil or be eaten by rats.

Falcon tore into his food like a famished wolf. He hadn't been so hungry since his last siege. As he stuffed venison into his mouth with one hand, he grabbed a handful of baked eggs from a passing tray with the other hand. Most of the other guests were eating with almost as much urgency, some had starved themselves for two days in order to do justice to this feast. It was some time before conversation resumed, and in the interim entertainment was provided. Besides the usual tumblers and jugglers and musicians, there were the king's prized freaks.

Among these were the "cocks." These were men, or possibly women, who had been mutilated in childhood for the purpose of providing amusement for the nobility. Their mouths had been slit back as far as the ears, and their lips trimmed to resemble beaks. Their vocal cords had been cut so that they could produce only crowing noises. Tricked out with red combs and with their arms encased in feathered "wings," they announced the hours by flapping and crowing, to the great amusement of the assembled guests. There were other entertainers equally grotesque.

Falcon took note of the guests at the high table. As before, the grand master of the temple sat near the king. Claude and Isabeau had places of honor. Gudrun was there, and so was Benedetto. Falcon smiled to see the two casting occasional venomous glances at each other. The others at the table he did not recognize.

He was sitting back, the worst of his hunger satisfied, when a steward appeared beside him. "Sir Draco Falcon?" the steward asked. Falcon nodded. "The king wishes the pleasure of your presence at his table."

Hugh looked over at him with eyebrows raised. "You're moving up in the world, Draco my boy. I'd just as soon stay here with my own kind, myself." Hugh took a long swallow of his wine. "Damn all kings, anyway." He did not say this last loud enough for anybody but Falcon to hear.

Falcon stood, glad now that he had spent his time so far eating instead of drinking. Eyes followed him as he made his way to the high table. He was not quite sure what he was supposed to do when he got there. As it occurred, there was nothing to worry about. A steward seated him at the table between two of the guests, who made way for him as at any other table.

Everyone was speaking of the tourney. Of about five hundred knights who had participated, some sixty-three had been killed, at least twice that many wounded with varying degrees of severity, and a number ruined through having to pay ransom. The campground, barriers, part of the stands, and much of the nearby village had been destroyed. All agreed that it had been many years since such a fine tourney had been seen.

Claude seemed embarrassed that so much was being made of his part in the fighting. Isabeau was clearly delighting in her role as Queen of Love and Beauty. "No, no," Claude was saying to someone, "the last charge wasn't my idea, it was Sir Draco's. I just went along with him and Sir Hugh because I didn't want to get left behind."

"Ah, that charge!" said a high noble. "It was one of the most foolish things I have ever seen, but done with such panache! It's good to see young men throw away their lives for the sake of style. Anybody can die in some common fashion."

"Sir Draco," called the king, "be so good as to come sit by me." He turned to the grand master, who was seated at his elbow. "Good master of the Temple, I pray you exchange places with Sir Draco for a while. I have matters to discuss with him."

"Of a surety, sire," said the grand master, rising. He seemed to have not the slightest apprehension that Falcon had matters concerning the Temple to report. That was a relief. Falcon had been fearing that the knight who had spoken to him in the hall of the Temple might have seen him at the tourney and recognized him as the warrior "student."

"Sir Draco," the king began, "please accept my thanks for your exemplary display at this tourney. But for your exceptional feats of arms, it might have been a rather ordinary event. The fact that you declined the championship in favor of Sir Claude only adds to your honor."

"My liege does me too much honor," Falcon said, wondering where this deluge of fulsome compliments was leading. He had no doubt that Philip had some sort of business in mind.

"Tell me, Sir Draco," said Philip, "I have heard that you possess an army of your own, that you hire out to divers employers for pay. Is this so?"

"It's true, sire." Falcon answered.

"That's most ingenious." The king looked at Falcon. One of Philip's eyes stared off at an angle from the other, but his gaze was no less acute for that. "How did you get such a unique idea?"

"There's really nothing new about it," Falcon said. "I was practically raised from boyhood in Palestine, and soldiering for hire has been common there for a century."

"I can see its advantages," Philip said. "I've always had to depend on my barons' feudal service for soldiers. I wish I could tell you how many campaigns I've lost just because, at the moment I had my enemy in my grasp, my barons decided that their forty days' service was up and they took their men and went home." He snorted. "Most of them can't count to forty. Look at them." The king gestured toward the assembled nobility with a half-gnawed duck leg. "Hardly a man of them but would cut my throat if it was to his slightest advantage."

"With a professional standing army, serving for pay, you would not have these problems, sire," Falcon pointed out.

"I've thought of that often, Sir Draco. To have an army at my command all year round, to be able to conduct sieges without regard to feudal obligation—this is how the old Romans gained and kept an empire, not with amateur landlords in armor, but with real soldiers!" Falcon wondered whether Philip was about to offer him a position in some kind of new royal army, but decided to wait and let events develop as they might.

"Do you know what the problem is, Sir Draco? Can you guess what keeps me from forming just such an army as we are discussing?"

Falcon thought for a moment. "Money."

"Exactly. It's not that I lack wealth, of course." He waved airily at the lavish surroundings. "It's the constant lack of coin. You can't pay an army in goats and bushels of wheat and expect it to march anywhere you say instantly. We're all tied too close to the land, Sir Draco."

"Perhaps, sire, your first course should be to reform the coinage," Falcon said.

"That's very true," Philip said, nodding, "but have you any idea how difficult that is? All my predecessors have increased the apparent size of their treasuries by adulterating the coinage—melting it down and alloying it with more and more base metal to stretch the gold and silver. It does no good. By some mysterious process the prices of everything go up and it pours from the treasury as swiftly as before."

"The burdens of kingship are awesome," Falcon commiserated.

"Now, I can call in all the coin of the realm and melt it down and reinstitute rigid standards of purity in the metal. It's easy to do. I have master coiners as good as the caliph's. Do you know what happens to the coins that are guaranteed pure?"

"What, sire?"

Philip threw up his hands in frustration. "They disappear! People hoard them. They bury them in the ground or in walls. The nobles and wealthy merchants melt them down and cast them into plate or gold thread for their garments, to show off their wealth. They embellish their armor, they decorate their sword hilts, they have it made into jewelry to decorate their wives, they do anything with it except spend it or pay their taxes!" Philip sat back in his chair after this outburst. He pushed his crown back, and Falcon saw that the king's hair was already beginning to go thin. It was not surprising.

"Sire," Falcon said, "I have read that the old Romans of whom you speak used to strike a special coin just for the purpose of paying soldiers. In fact, the coin was called a *solidus*, and it was from this that we have the word 'soldier.' "

"In truth?" the king said. "That would be convenient, if the money went first of all to pay the troops. They would use it quickly instead of hoarding it."

"And," Falcon went on, "if they were kept in royal garrisons, where you owned or taxed most of the local trades and lands, much of that money would return to you directly."

"This bears thinking about," Philip said, stroking his beard.

"Think also of this," Falcon continued. "Soldiers are simple men. Most of their pay can be in silver and copper. Many a soldier never touches gold in all his life unless it be loot."

"That is very wise, Sir Draco. But there is still the problem of the leaders of these men. Noblemen are hard to find that would be willing to leave their lands for long periods, and they would not come cheap."

"You put too high a value on birth, sire," Falcon chided. "It is known to all that you keep a council of men of humble birth but much wisdom to advise you in civil matters. Why should war be different?"

The king frowned, deep in thought. "Commoners, to lead men in battle? I don't know, Sir Draco. That might be going too far."

"Then, sire, look for your leaders among the younger sons."

"The cadets?" Philip said. "This is something to ponder on. That would be a good use to put them to, by God!"

Falcon smiled and nodded. One of the great problems of the feudal system was that only one son could inherit the family property, but all sons were raised to

134

be warriors and leaders, in case the oldest died before producing an heir. The result was a great mob of young men with no lands and no prospects who were trained to nothing but war. It had produced a sizable corps of troublemakers who often turned bandit to live. These younger sons were known as cadets.

"Sir Draco, you are a man of rare gifts," the king said. "You are a great warrior, but I have many such. You can read, and I have few men who can do that. You seem to understand money, and I have nobody at all who can make that claim. Besides this, you have some new ideas about organizing an army. Sir Draco, I am prepared to offer you a place with me. Will you join my council of advisers?"

Falcon was torn between elation and dread. Here was a chance to make himself great. Here was a chance to regain his family lands, at least when Philip retook Normandy, which had to be soon. Then other thoughts intruded. He saw himself spending years in cramped royal offices going over tax rolls and pay rolls, attending endless advisory councils and, worst of all, having to live among the kind of flattering, back-stabbing courtiers he saw all about him here tonight.

"My lord overwhelms me with his favor," Falcon said, "but I fear I must decline."

"Whatever for?" asked Philip pettishly. "First you decline the championship of the tourney, then you refuse an honor anyone else here would cheerfully boil a rival in oil to receive."

Falcon thought hard. It could be deadly to refuse royal favor. He decided to be truthful and to appeal to the basic savage who dwelled in the breast of any feudal noble, be he baron or king.

"Sire, to be your man would be my greatest desire, but I have a vengeance to accomplish."

"Vengeance?" said Philip, intrigued.

"Yes. In Palestine, my father was betrayed, tortured, and killed by four men. I swore a holy oath to kill those men. I have killed one, but three still live, and neither I nor my father's spirit can know rest until the other three are dead at my feet."

"Admirable, admirable," Philip said, nodding his head. "But, Sir Draco, I am a liberal monarch, and I treat my vassals well. If you take service with me, you need merely name these three varlets and I'll clap 'em in the dungeon and give you the key."

"Sire," Falcon said, "if they were within your domains, I would accept your offer without demur. However, I fear that they are not. One is an English earl, another a Flemish churchman, the third a Norman like myself."

The king brooded awhile, then: "Sir Draco, while I grieve to lose the services of so unusual a man as yourself, I cannot find it in me to condemn a man who wishes to avenge his father. All my life, I have desired to wreak vengeance upon those who betrayed *my* father, but I was constrained by the fact that those persons were appointed kings and queens. I envy your ability to take your revenge with a few good sword strokes. I accept your reasons for declining my service, and I wish you good hunting."

"Your highness is too kind. If I may make a suggestion . . ."

"Yes?" Philip asked.

"It strikes me that many of your troubles stem from having no one who is skilled at handling money. There are already those within your kingdom who have this skill, persons who are not forbidden as are Christians from trafficking in money and causing it to multiply."

"You mean the Jews?" The king frowned. "I fear

not, Sir Draco. My other counselors would never submit to having unbelievers high in my service."

"Your highness has brought those barons to heel before this," Falcon pointed out.

"This would be too much. Were it not for the spirit of the Crusade, I might take your advice. However, just now the Hebrews are doing well to keep their lives, much less gain royal favor. In these days, any coward who would fear to go to Palestine and fight, as you and I did, will cut down some defenseless Jew in the street and proclaim himself a soldier of Christ."

"Crusading is growing as debased as the coinage," Falcon observed. The king threw back his head and roared with laughter. None of the others had heard what Falcon said, but a number of the courtiers laughed anyway, just to be safe.

Suddenly, the king turned serious. "There are those here, Sir Draco, who would have themselves in control of the kingdom's finances." He sent a pointed look toward the grand master of the Temple, who was in animated conversation with an old baron at his side. Here was his opening at last.

"As it occurs, sire," Falcon said, "I wish to speak with you about the Temple. It is a matter of some urgency."

"The Temple?" Philip said, then suddenly, "Oh, I'm tired of all this talk about money and armies and the Temple! Tell us of your adventures in Palestine, Sir Draco. Were you at Hattin?"

"I was, sire. But, if you please, sire, the Templars—"

"I do not please!" Philip barked. "I've talked enough statecraft for tonight. Let's hear some rousing tales of Outremer!"

Falcon gritted his teeth. Philip's new animation had attracted the attention of others at the table, and a private conversation was impossible. Philip, like most great lords Falcon had known, had a childish streak. Brilliant as he was, he was easily distracted and had difficulty in keeping his mind on serious business for long. Falcon would have to wait for a more propitious occasion. Resignedly, he launched into one of his more elaborate lies about his adventures.

TEN

THE TARGET was forty paces away. Falcon raised his
Saracen bow, arrow nocked to string. On his thumb
was a ring made of rhinoceros horn. He hooked the
silken string on the ring and locked his thumb with
his forefinger. The ring took the bite of the string as
he drew it to his right ear and took careful aim. His
finger released the thumb, and the string slid from the
smooth ring and flew forward, propelling the arrow
toward the target. The shaft sank into the canvas
stretched over the tight-woven straw about five inches
to the right of the painted bull's-eye.

"You've not practiced in too long," Wulf said.

"I know," Falcon answered. He took up another arrow. The butts, or targets, were set up behind the
palace for the practice of the royal archers of the
guards. The archers were admiring Falcon's shot.
Their own bows were of the traditional type: made
of a single piece of wood and drawn only to the

breast. Falcon's Saracen bow was made of strips of wood, horn, and sinew layered and glued together into a spring of extreme resilience and power. The shot had been more accurate than most of the king's archers could have managed, and the Saracen bow was capable of casts greatly in excess of those of the wooden bows.

He turned at the sound of hoofbeats and saw two riders approaching. One was Gudrun, the other a man he did not recognize. Falcon took up another arrow and nocked it. He drew and took aim. This one struck three inches to the left of the other.

"That's better," Wulf said.

"Sir Draco," Gudrun said, "surely that isn't a very knightly pastime."

"In Outremer, lady," Falcon said, "it's a common knightly accomplishment. Often the Saracens refuse to commit suicide by riding out for sword strokes with Frankish knights. Instead, they keep their distance and shoot arrows at us. The only way to fight them is to shoot likewise." He shot again, and this time he struck dead center.

"Bull's-eye!" Wulf said.

"Excellent, Sir Draco," said the man who accompanied Gudrun. He was dressed in the plain but well-cut clothes of a valued chamberlain of less than noble birth.

"This is René Croix," Gudrun said. "He is a seneschal of the Viscount of Limoges and says that he has been combing Paris looking for you."

"So, you're the man I came here to meet," Falcon said.

"Indeed. I feared that something had befallen you when I could not locate you. But Paris is a very large city, and I persevered. Then I heard that the hero of the royal tourney was Sir Draco Falcon. Lady

Gudrun found me as I was questioning my fifth royal steward of the day, and she kindly offered to guide me to you."

"I thank you, my lady," Falcon said with a bow. "The gentleman and I have some business to discuss."

"Yes, I know." Gudrun said. "I will not hinder your discussion. However, Sir Draco, tomorrow there is to be a royal hunt in the wood to the east. I shall need an escort. Would you favor me with your company?"

Falcon smiled wryly. She had him neatly trapped. She had brought him the man he had been searching for, and it would be churlish for him to refuse. "It will be my honor," he answered.

"Sir Draco," said René Croix when they were alone, "as you understood from the message sent to you, my lord the Viscount of Limoges has a task that will require a sizable body of trained fighting men who are free to travel as they will within France."

"And the nature of this service?" Falcon asked.

René Croix glanced suspiciously at Wulf. "Perhaps, sir, this should be for your ears alone."

"Wulf is my right arm," Falcon said. "We have shared everything since we were boys, including secrets. Tell me what you're hiring me for."

"Well, then, as you and the rest of the world have heard by now, the late King Richard of England died during a dispute with my lord."

"I've so heard," Falcon confirmed.

"Do you know what the dispute was about?"

"Some say that it was over a treasure trove that both men claimed."

"That is quite so. Some peasants found a great hoard of gold while plowing land in dispute between my lord and King Richard. Of course, my lord's claim was just, while that of Richard was spurious, and it served him right to catch a bolt during his felonious raid."

"I was no friend of Richard," Falcon said. "Go on."

"My lord now holds this treasure in his castle at Limoges. He wishes to transfer it to the castle of Cahors, held for him at this time by a cousin. He wishes you to escort this treasure with your army."

"What's wrong with his own?" Falcon asked.

"You and your men may travel freely, since you have no lord. My lord's men would have to pass through hostile territory."

"Why do you think we can protect this treasure? Richard came after it with his whole army. I have only two hundred men."

"Word has carefully been spread that the treasure never existed, that King Richard was merely chasing a rumor. None will know that you and your men are carrying anything so valuable. The only danger will be from outlaws of the type that commonly prey upon travelers. Your force will be more than sufficient to deal with these."

"It'll mean breaking winter quarters and bringing my men to Limoges. Then we must march for days across the mountains of Auvergne in the dead of winter. All my force is mounted, and feed for the horses will be skimpy."

"My lord will provide wagons for fodder for your mounts. For the rest, I can assure you that you will be most generously recompensed for your effort."

"Be sure that I will require that," Falcon said. "Agreed." He saw Wulf wince slightly, but the Saxon was holding his peace, for now.

They agreed upon an approximate date for Falcon and his little army to arrive at Limoges, and then they parted company. As soon as René was gone, Wulf began his tirade.

"Escorting treasure!" Wulf said. "No matter what that sheep-counter says, the word'll get out!"

"He says that most think it was just a rumor."

"That rumor got Richard killed. Where gold is concerned, men don't waste much thought on likelihood. If the word spreads that we've got that treasure with us, we'll have every bandit and robber baron between the Rhine and the Pyrenees after us."

"You worry too much, Wulf," Falcon said.

"And what of your own men?" Wulf went on, as if he'd said nothing. "They're only plain soldiers. How many of them would you trust if they suspect that there's enough gold in the chests to make them all rich men?"

"None," Falcon said. "So we'll have to be very quiet about it, won't we?"

"And they'll be in a bad humor anyway," Wulf proceeded relentlessly, "because they'll have to travel in winter."

"Isn't that one of the reasons I built this army in the first place? So we could campaign in any season? So far, they've sat on their collective buttocks in winter quarters, eating our stores and earning no pay. It's time they started learning how to soldier as professionals instead of as a feudal levy."

"I don't like it," Wulf said stubbornly.

"You never do," Falcon said, "so shut up."

For the hunt, Falcon was given a courser from the royal stables. This was a fleet-footed beast bred for long chases. He wore plain dark-green hose and soft boots, and over his green shirt he wore a sleeveless jerkin of brown leather. Around his waist he had belted his dagger and Nemesis. It was not customary to bear weapons of war while hunting, but Falcon regarded himself as a soldier first and foremost, and he was in territory he did not control, and that meant enemy territory.

In any case, Falcon was not fond of hunting. His lack of enthusiasm was regarded by his peers as something of a betrayal of his class, for most nobles and knights were as passionate about hunting as they were about fighting. Falcon's father had been a fanatic about hunting. It was with the lure of a lion hunt that his betrayers had led him to his death. That may have been part of the reason Falcon did not care for hunting. Mainly, though, he found it boring. To him, hunting was a task which was sometimes necessary in order to have meat. When he was with his men, Falcon left the hunting to his archers and crossbowmen, who could go out and stock the larder without endangering men, dogs, or horses. The peerage, on the other hand, could make a hunt as dangerous as war or tourney. Like everything else, they liked their sport rough and perilous.

The hunt was assembling outside the city walls near where the tourney had been held. To his surprise, few of those assembled were dressed in plain, practical hunting clothes like his own. Instead, they were attired as colorfully as for a court ball. The silks and hose were of all hues, and the men wore caps with long feathers drooping from them. Most of the men wore short hunting swords, about as impractical as any weapons could be. Too long for use as hunting knives, and too short to be effective for fighting, they served only as an advertisement that the bearer was sufficiently well bred to hunt and bear arms.

The ladies were dressed as gaily. The whole event looked like the first outing of May, an incongruous sight beneath the lowering October sky. There was a knot of huntsmen leading dogs, and others with long poles and nets. Lady Gudrun caught sight of him and waved him over. The king was not there yet. As protocol dictated, he would be last to arrive, and his appearance would signal the beginning of the hunt.

"Sir Draco," Gudrun said, "come join us." Unlike the other ladies, who rode gentle palfreys, Gudrun was mounted on a spirited courser. She was wearing a rust-colored gown and had dispensed with her coif and wimple, instead letting her white-blond hair flow free, the thick locks braided with strings of red, brown, and yellow leaves. Among the fluttering court ladies she stood out like a heroic statue among funeral effigies.

A huntsman went about passing out spears. Falcon took one, and so did Gudrun. She handled it expertly, which came as no surprise to Falcon. The spear told him what they were hunting. It had a stout shaft about nine feet long; its head was extraordinarily broad; and a foot below the head was a crossbar, all of which meant that they were hunting boar. A wild boar was the most dangerous animal in the West, and it could be far deadlier than any lion. It was capable of being impaled on a spear and then forcing its way up the shaft to gut the spearman with its tusks. The crossbar was to prevent this.

"Good sport today, Sir Draco," said one of the men who were conversing with Gudrun. "There's a big boar in the woods over near the Temple. It's killed a couple of villeins already and we're going after it."

"After all," said another happily, "it's our duty to protect the villagers." Falcon refrained from laughing. The peasants could have disposed of the beast efficiently, but they were forbidden to protect themselves thus, because hunting was reserved for the nobles. The boar could go on killing them all winter and they would have to wait until some wellborn pig-sticker showed up to skewer the animal.

The king arrived at last, and they all trooped off behind him. By late morning they were in the woods, and the king's huntsmen fanned out with their dogs to look for sign of the boar, returning shortly to report their progress. One bore a few hog bristles. Another held his cupped palms up to the king. His hands were full of fewmets, as droppings were called in hunter's jargon. The king examined them closely, and his companions discussed the significance of these specimens.

"Surely," Falcon said to Gudrun, "the King of France has better things to do than poke around in pig shit."

"You do not enjoy the mysteries of the hunter's craft?" Gudrun asked.

"I've spent too much time as a hunted man to enjoy the hunting of beasts," he answered.

"You were hunted?" Gudrun asked with interest. "Is that how you got that back covered with scars? I wondered. It was like running my hands over a field plowed by elves."

"No," he said, "that is the mark of time I spent as a beast in chains. I take no delight in caged animals, either." How could anyone here understand what it was like to pull an oar as a chained slave? Their imaginations were not that flexible. They would plunge their spears into the boar and see in it no reflection of their own probable deaths, writhing on the spear of some enemy knight.

He tried to shake off the foul mood, brought on by his disgust with the court and with city life in general. Cities were places for soldiers to squander their loot between battles, and courts were places for ambitious nobles to plot and devise treacherous schemes. He had no other use for them, and he longed to return to his soldiers, to the fields and the castles and the open country.

They rode to a clump of heavy brush where the huntsmen had determined that the boar was hiding. The nets were hung from the poles all around the copse, to contain the boar when it charged. Philip dismounted, for by custom he had the first try at the beast. If he failed, the others could try in strict order of precedence. Philip strode to the net and signaled to the huntsmen to begin. He showed a kingly disdain of his danger, but Falcon could see the white of the knuckles that held the spear. Falcon hoped that the net was strong enough to hold the beast while Philip planted his spear.

There was an explosion of snorting and squealing as the huntsmen thrust long poles into the copse. The boar burst out and planted its small, sharp hooves, glaring about with little red eyes to find its tormentors. The party gasped and muttered at the size of the animal. It was as big as any boar Falcon had ever seen and black as night, with tusks that curved upward from its lower jaw for nearly a foot. Those tusks, hooking up from below, were almost impossible to defend against.

At the side of his vision, something drew Falcon's attention. He turned and saw two men, dressed as huntsmen, slowly drawing away from the party. They saw him looking at them, and they turned and ran at full speed down a forest path. Falcon heard a great cry from the hunters as the boar made his charge, then he was spurring his horse toward the king. Somebody shouted at this *lèse-majesté*, then all fell silent in horror as the boar reached the net and went through it as if it had been a spider web.

Philip's spear took the boar just in front of the left shoulder, and it penetrated as far as the crossbar. The king was hurled back by the force of the charge, and the boar began to shake him on the shaft like a rag puppet. The king was truly holding on for his life, for to let go now would be his death. Then Falcon reined in beside the animal and thrust his spear into its side. The boar's struggles pulled the spear from his hand, and he dismounted, drawing his sword. He swung the curved blade, but succeeded only in opening a cut in its shoulder. It was twisting too rapidly to get a good cut at its neck. The king lost one hand's grip on the spear, and then he was tumbling loose. The boar turned toward him with its great gutting tusks, and then Gudrun was leaping her courser over the creature, leaning down from her saddle like a Valkyrie to plunge her spear into its back. The beast stiffened with shock for a bare moment and gave Falcon the opportunity he needed. He brought Nemesis down with both hands in a huge arc, striking with the section of blade near the hilt, bearing down and drawing back at the same time to make the longest possible cut.

The bristles that lay across the back of the neck were as tough as mail. But the blade sheared through to the thick, tough muscle on the back of the boar's neck, then through the bones of the spine. After that, the neck parted easily, and the massive, fierce head thumped to the ground. The body stood for another moment, then collapsed, spurting blood and spinal fluid and stomach contents into a noisome pool on the ground. The carcass twitched for a few seconds, then lay still.

Servants and courtiers hastened to help Philip to his feet and dust him off. He stood as if nothing untoward had happened. "Now," Philip said, "we don't have sport like that every day, do we?" He looked over to where Falcon was standing, wiping the blood from his sword with a scrap of cloth. "My thanks, Sir Draco," he called. He strode up to Falcon and said in a slightly lower voice: "How did you get to my side so quickly?"

"I saw two varlets dressed as huntsmen running away as the boar broke cover. I suspected—" Then Philip was clapping him on the shoulder hard enough to silence him.

"It's good to have men around who are alert and swift. And Lady Gudrun, too. Where is she?" Gudrun was riding back into the small clearing. Her horse was snorting and rolling its eyes at the smell of the boar's blood.

"I got him to leap the boar readily enough," she said, "but I had a hard time stopping him once he was on the other side."

"You were splendid, my lady," Philip pronounced. "It was like something from an old tale."

Gudrun smiled sunnily, and the other ladies glowered to be outshone by this statuesque Amazon. Her color was high and her leaf-strewn hair swirled wildly around her elbows. All the men watched her with undisguised admiration, and this further darkened the ladies' looks. Bull's-eye! Falcon thought. She'll be wringing poor Philip out tonight for certain. Before morning he'll be wishing he'd taken his chances with the boar.

Falcon mounted, and two riders came over to congratulate him. All the others clustered around Gudrun. The two were Claude de Coucy and Isabeau. He had not realized that they were with the hunt, because, feeling out of place in the glittering assemblage, they had ridden on the edge of the group. He had a strong suspicion that they had slipped off into the woods at some time for their own kind of sport.

"This seems to be your destiny, Sir Draco," said Claude. "Always you are the hero and somebody else steals your glory."

"Glory is for poems and tales," Falcon said, "and royal favor is fleeting and treacherous. Have nothing to do with either if you can help it, Claude."

"That's just what I've been telling him, Sir Draco," Isabeau said. "In fact, I'd just like to go home so we can be married."

"Take her advice, Claude," Falcon said. "Leave this place. I'd go myself, except—well, I have business that detains me at the court, but not for much longer."

"I thought it might seem churlish to go so soon after the king proclaimed me champion," Claude maintained.

"She's champion now," Falcon said, indicating Gudrun with his chin.

"She was magnificent, don't you think?" Isabeau said. Falcon smiled slightly. Here was one lady at least who had no fear that her man was lusting after Gudrun.

"Why did the net part like that?" Claude asked.

"King Philip doesn't seem to be puzzled by the occurrence, does he?" Falcon queried. The couple looked to where Philip was in animated conversation with Gudrun, the courtiers fawning on them both.

"Why, no," Isabeau said. "He's acting as if it were an ordinary mishap."

"Then I suggest that you both follow his example." By their expressions, he could tell that the happy couple had come to the realization that court life was something far different from what they had expected.

During the ride back to the palace, Philip talked volubly about trifles, but at one point he sent a courtier to invite Falcon to dinner at the palace that night.

This banquet was far smaller than the one after the tourney. The great majority of those who had been in Paris for the tourney had left in order to get home before the worst of the winter weather struck. Even so, it was a lavish affair, with many courses and much entertainment, with knights declaiming in loud voices and wretched verse the story of Gudrun's feat that day. Falcon rated a few lines as the man who had given the beast its *coup de grace*.

The animal itself arrived as the main course, its great head with its fearsome tusks gracing a separate platter. Draco ate his share with great relish. He had to admit it: There was something immensely satisfying about eating a beast that had been about to kill him. He was not alone in this feeling, for he noticed that Philip and Gudrun were tearing away with similar gusto. But then, Gudrun always glutted her appetites for food, wine, and men as if they guaranteed her eternal youth.

The grand master was not there, and Falcon could not remember having seen him at the hunt that day. It probably meant nothing. He was developing a habit of reading dark meanings into everything concerning the Temple. Claude and Isabeau sat at the lower table, of which there was only one now. In a similar reduction of the previously lavish scale, there was one sole salt cellar, and this sat before the king. It was passed among the guests at the high table, then those who sat below the salt had their turn.

The king rose and retired early, and Falcon guessed that Philip was hot to be after Gudrun. Therefore, he was amazed when a servant summoned him to the king's privy chamber as he was preparing to leave the palace.

He found Philip sitting at a table dressed in a light sleeping gown. Without his crown and royal robes he looked frail, and the light of a single candle before him was not kind, but made a deep shadow of every line in the man's face. With his thinning hair, he looked like a man approaching sixty. If this was what kingly power did to a man, Falcon thought, then he wanted none of it. Philip gestured for him to sit, and Falcon seated himself on a chest. The king sat on the room's only chair.

"Sir Draco," Philip began, "I will make this brief, for I have—other matters to attend to this night." Draco said nothing, as nothing seemed called for. "I hope you understand," Philip went on, "that I know quite well that it was you who saved my life today. The Lady Gudrun's deed was splendid and worthy of a heroine, but she merely helped you finish the brute. Also, you must understand that I silenced you when you were about to acquaint me with what you saw because there are some things that should not be common knowledge."

"My liege has no need to explain to me. I am a poor knight, and the great affairs of state are far above me."

Philip smiled wryly. "And modest, too, I see. Sir Draco, you are an intriguing rogue, but I find that I like you. Now, finish what you were about to tell me at the tourney banquet. Tell me about the Temple."

Falcon took a deep breath. Philip waited attentively. Briefly, with few words, he told the king of his suspicions of the Temple, of his penetration of its defenses disguised as a student, of the conversation he had overheard, of his interpretation of those words, of his taking part in the tourney to gain the king's ear.

"So, you think the Temple had some part in your father's betrayal?" asked Philip, when the story was over.

"Perhaps not the Temple, but at least the former grand master, Gerard."

"Sir Draco, you have brought me a tale of a few nebulous words—the red one, the landless one, the great one. On another occasion I might have thrown you from the palace as a slanderer and a madman. However, I have had my own suspicions of the Temple for some time. And there was the incident of the boar this morning." He regarded Falcon levelly.

"I had the huntsmen assembled after we returned to the city," he went on. "My master huntsman reported two missing. I told him to locate them or lose his head. He went back to the hunting site with a pack of dogs and all the trackers of the royal hunting establishment. Just before dinner he returned. They had found the two men in a ditch with their throats cut. Their clothing had been stolen." Philip took a swallow from a winecup that sat on the table before him.

"The net had been cut, of course, not in one place but in many. The two dead men were the ones detailed to carry the net. Nobody noticed when they were replaced by the conspirators, but then, why should they?" He leaned back in his chair and looked Falcon in the eye.

"Sir Draco," he said, "by your actions today, you and Lady Gudrun are the only persons I can be sure had no part in this plot against my life. All the rest stood staring."

"I am sure that all were stuck to the spot by dismay," Falcon said.

"Most, certainly, but probably not all. You are as swift as any man I have ever seen, and you have that sword that seems to leap into your hand when you need it and to strike by itself.

"Sir Draco, I know that you have obligations of great import to you, but I must ask that you act as my bodyguard until I have broken this conspiracy."

"I could do you little good, sire," Falcon said. "If your enemies see me dogging your every step they will simply try to get at you some other way. There is always poison, you know."

"I have tasters for that. In any case, you will not be seen to be my guard. Just stay nearby for a few days. Have that sword handy. It will seem natural. Lady Gudrun will be with me, as well, and that young de Coucy fellow. You will appear to be my latest favorites."

"You'd trust Claude?" Falcon said. "He was going to become a Templar."

"That's why I want him where I can see him. I don't think he's connected. After all, you say he was cuddling the floor while all that plotting at the Temple was going on, and in any case it was chance that made him champion of the tourney and put him in the palace. The boy seems open and honest as a spring lamb. However, I cannot be absolutely sure he was not planted on me."

"The boy wants to go home and marry his lass. Just give him your leave and have your men make sure that he has left Paris."

"I think not," the king said. "He may not be an assassin, but it is possible that he is here as a spy, to report on my movements. If that is true, I want to have him when I discover the rest of the traitors."

"As you say, sire." Poor Claude, Falcon thought.

"Sir Draco, you have my leave. Attend me tomorrow. Now I have more pleasant things to attend to."

Falcon bowed. That's what you think, he thought.

ELEVEN

WULF STARED about him. This was his first visit to the palace. His falchion and his little shield were hooked to his belt, and he wore his mailshirt and steel cap. "The ceiling's pretty," he said, "and the tapestries are fine, but we've seen finer palaces in Palestine."

Wulf was determined not to be impressed with the palace or with Falcon's new position as royal bodyguard. He wanted to be away there and back with the men. Falcon wanted the same thing, but he had to put a good face on things.

Philip invited Falcon to join him at breakfast, and Falcon found him sitting in the privy chamber, a trencher of ham and bread before him. The king looked as if he had spent the night tumbling repeatedly down the palace stairs. He raised his bloodshot eyes as Falcon entered and gestured for him to sit and share the royal trencher.

As Falcon did so, Philip spotted Wulf loitering in the hallway outside. "Who is that man?"

"That's Wulf. We've been together since we were boys in Palestine. He shared a bench with me on the Turkish galley. You can trust him without stint. And if you think I'm fast, you should see him in action."

"Good, then," Philip said. He seemed to have few words this morning. They finished the last of the meat and bread and their mugs of weak morning ale. Philip began to rise, and Falcon stood.

"Await me outside in the hall while I dress for my morning audience, Sir Draco."

Falcon had turned to go when Philip said: "Sir Draco." He turned. Philip was looking at him with eyes that looked a hundred years old. "Beware the Germans, Sir Draco," he warned. "If they ever become civilized, the world will be in great danger." Falcon bowed at this sage advice and left to await without.

The day passed without incident, and Falcon found himself hard pressed to cope with his boredom. Fortunately, Philip retired early. It seemed that he had had little sleep the night before. Falcon found a palace room where churchmen were quartered and asked after the whereabouts of Fra Benedetto. He was told of an inn next to the palace where the Italian clergyman had taken lodging.

As he might have expected, Benedetto had rented the entire upper floor of the inn for himself and his servants. The door opened at his knock, and Falcon entered, looking about at the large, loftlike room that occupied the upper floor. The furnishings were sparse, but Benedetto had brought his traveling chests, and the single bed was covered with rich bedclothes.

"Ah, Sir Draco, welcome," Benedetto said. "I've been wondering when you would show up."

"Matters have detained me thus far," Falcon said. He accepted the cup of wine a servant offered. "How has your task been progressing?"

Benedetto shrugged. "I lost a round yesterday. While I seek access to Philip's privy chamber, the Alemannic Jezebel gains his bedchamber. No matter. The temptations she offers will lose their savor in time, and I shall again have my opportunity.

"Now, what brings you to me? Somehow, I suspect that you do not wish to be shriven."

"I find myself in the midst of events over which I have no control and which I cannot understand. I'm a soldier and I fight for whoever pays me, within certain limits. Almost always, it's some baron who is fighting a neighbor, and the issues and motives are simple: land, treasure, someone's injured honor."

"And now," Benedetto said, "you are at court, where nothing is quite as it seems, where those who are most cordial to one another are the deadliest enemies, where a king's smile is something to kill for, and maneuvers conducted at a banquet are as momentous as those on a battlefield."

"That is the case," Falcon admitted.

"And what might be the nature of the events which so concern you?"

Falcon thought awhile before answering. He tried to remember Abraham's lessons in debate and statecraft: how to use as few words and reveal as little as possible while extracting the information he needed. "Let us say," he began, "just as an exercise in speculation, that someone were plotting against a certain king."

"Then we would know very little," said Benedetto, "for kings live in a constant welter of plots every day of their lives."

"But suppose this plot originated from a most unexpected source," Falcon persisted.

"Where else do plots originate?" Benedetto parried. "One is never in doubt about those likely to plot against one. It is always the unlikely sources that bear watching."

Benedetto was certainly not making this easy. He was not about to part with any advice until he had been given something first.

"Imagine," Falcon hazarded, "that a certain group of men, wealthy and powerful, respected throughout Christendom, were, against all seeming logic, planning the death of a certain monarch who has been their strong supporter?" Benedetto sat for a while and said nothing. Then he told his servants to leave. When they were gone he turned once more to Falcon.

"We need bandy words no longer, Sir Draco. You are saying that the Temple plots the death of King Philip, are you not?"

"I have not said that," Falcon protested.

"Just so."

"However, were you to draw that conclusion, I would not be vehement in my denial."

"You should have been an Italian, Sir Draco. I had noticed today that you never strayed far from Philip, even though you had few words with his inner circle. You are not a courtier, and it is clear that you have no ambitions to be one. I take it then that you are acting as the king's bodyguard?"

"He is impressed with my martial alacrity. He wishes to have it at his disposal in these trying times."

"Philip is a sagacious man. Sir Draco, have you any idea what has driven the Templars to such a desperate measure?"

"I tried to puzzle it out. I know how rich they are.

I know that they are ambitious and that Philip is the only king powerful enough to defy them at this time, but it still seems a poor reason, especially since he probably owes them a great deal of money and his successor might not honor the debt."

"There is far more at stake in this than the payment of the debt. The very future of the Temple is at stake, and has been for some time."

"How is this?" Falcon asked.

"You went to the Crusade as a very young man, is that not so?"

"It is."

"How great were the Crusader kingdoms when you arrived in Palestine?"

"They were large, although not as great as they had been. There was the Kingdom of Jerusalem, the County of Edessa, the County of Tripoli, the Principality of Antioch, and a few smaller holdings. Edessa was almost gone before I arrived. The Seljuks had taken most of it back years before."

"And of what do those proud holdings consist now?"

"Last I heard," Draco said, "just a thin coastal strip and a few port cities."

"Precisely. The Temple existed to protect the pilgrim routes and prosecute the war against the Saracens. Now they have no reason to exist."

"Surely," Falcon protested, "there will be other Crusades. We have suffered a series of setbacks. Saladin is dead now. Soon the church will preach a Crusade and the knights will be marching again."

Benedetto shook his head slowly. "No, Sir Draco. Disabuse yourself of that notion. The great days of Crusading are over. In the beginning, the knights and others were an almost leaderless, planless mob, driven by faith, and they were victorious. You were in the most recent campaigns. They were the wars of kings and barons out to advance their own causes, and they ended in unmitigated disaster. It was just a brawl between princes transferred to Palestine."

Falcon had no argument with that. It was his own opinion, although it surprised him to hear a churchman say it.

"No," Benedetto went on, "the Holy Land is now in Saracen hands and likely to stay that way. This is not necessarily an evil thing. Look about you. What is the state of Christendom?"

"A chaotic shambles, as always." Falcon answered.

"I couldn't have said it better myself. Yes, the state of the West is a scandal. Until the Christian powers of Europe have sorted out their own problems they have no call to go adventuring off in the East." He took a sip of his wine, then continued. "There are political realities in this world, Sir Draco, that should not be confused with the longings of faith or the rewards of devotion."

"Men have been burned for talk like that," Falcon pointed out.

"In the past, yes, and probably in the future, but the new Holy Father is a man of realism as well as of faith. He has little love for the squabbling monarchs of Christendom, but he wants to see some sort of unity and stability come out of this confusion. Right now, the kings, princes, barons, and minor nobility see themselves as enemies of the Pope because they fear that he threatens their power. They are wrong in this. The power of the petty barons must be reduced, it is true, but the Holy Father is convinced that strong kings whose power is absolute within their domains would be a strong support for the throne of St. Peter. Right now, there are too many of them and their power is fleeting. There should be one for England and its islands; one for France, and by that I mean for all the French-speaking lands; one for Spain; and perhaps one for the German lands. With true nations instead of squabbling principalities, all united by the church, the West could once again regain preeminence in the world. At least, the Crusades have taught us that we dwell in a backward swamp."

"And what of the empire?" Falcon asked.

"An outdated concept," Benedetto said. "The old empire was held together by the Caesars and their armies. The church will unify the new one."

"Plans like this will take some time to mature," observed Falcon.

"Centuries, likely enough. No matter—the church has all the centuries it needs. Now, have you figured out just who stands to lose the most by the growing power of the kings and the papacy?"

"The Temple, of course. I had already had some glimmerings, but your words have shown how limited were my projections."

"With no reason for existence in the East, the Temple must gain all the power it can in the West. Already it has lands, strong castles, and riches. It has a corps of soldiers who are not distracted by the care of lands and who can own no property or power to be handed down by inheritance. All lands, property, and power remain within the control of the Temple, under the direction of the grand master, and the regional masters and chapters."

"Much like the church," Falcon said.

"Yes." Benedetto nodded. "Save that the church's authority is spiritual while that of the Temple is military. But only weak kings would allow those monster castles to squat upon their territories. Only rulers with no capacity to manage an exchequer would keep their treasure with what amounts to a foreign power. Strong rulers or a strong church would be a threat to the Temple's prosperity."

"So they want to do away with Philip."

Benedetto leaned back and steepled his fingers. He stared at the wall opposite with a brooding glare. "I greatly fear that Philip is not their only target."

Falcon's mind took a sudden leap. "The Pope?"

"Innocent III is probably the most capable man to hold the throne in generations. He is even more dangerous to them than Philip. Other things occur to me."

"Such as?" Falcon queried.

"Who has been the only emperor in this century to be of any real consequence?"

"Barbarossa," Falcon answered.

"That is right. Frederick Barbarossa, greatest emperor since Charlemagne. Ten years ago, he rode to the Crusade. As he neared the Holy Land, he drowned in a river. Not much of a death for a great warrior like Frederick, was it? Not very likely, either. Did you know that Frederick was riding with an escort of Templars when he died?"

"No," Falcon said, very slowly, "I didn't."

"I knew, but never until this night did I make the connection. Sir Draco, you have done the church a great favor."

"Unwittingly," Falcon said.

"Nevertheless, the Holy Father shall know of it."

"I need no gratitude from the Pope."

"Do not scorn it," Benedetto said. "The Holy Father can be a powerful friend at need." Falcon merely shrugged. "I must be off to Rome," Benedetto continued. "The Pope must be apprised of this situation immediately."

"What of your mission to advance the cause of Philip of Swabia? Or was it Otto of Brunswick?"

"These are petty matters now," Benedetto said. "Let Gudrun have her way for now. Philip's a willful man and will choose as he thinks best in any case. And now, Sir Draco, I must beg your leave. I have some packing to do."

Falcon's next stop was at the Two Swords. The students clapped and shouted to see him and Wulf when they came through the door. Mika and some others rose to greet them.

"Sir Draco! Wulf! Come sit and have some ale. We'd thought you gone from Paris days ago. Is it true you won the tourney single-handed?"

"Almost," Falcon answered. He looked the young Finn over. Like most of the students present, Mika had acquired several new cuts and bruises. There must have been another riot. After a few mugs of ale and some exchanged pleasantries, Falcon came to the point. "Mika, what happened at the Temple after I left?"

"Some very boring lectures."

"No, I mean that night and the next morning."

"Well, there was a good deal of rushing about and searching, but that wasn't for you, it was for some novice who had disappeared. They questioned us about two students who had left that night, but of course we knew nothing. That was all."

"I had hoped for more," Falcon said, brooding into his ale.

"Wait," said one of the students. "What about that pack of brigands who came riding in just as we were leaving?"

"Oh, yes, I'd forgotten them," Mika said. "There

were at least twenty of them. They wore Templar white, but they looked foreign. Most of them were dark and they rode horses that were smaller than most knights ride. They were a tough-looking band, lots of scars, and armed to the teeth."

"Thank you," Falcon said. "That may be helpful."

"Helpful for what?" Mika asked.

"Be glad that you don't know," Falcon said.

He found Claude de Coucy in a room of the palace which he shared with several other bachelor knights. Isabeau and her servants were in the ladies' section on the other side of the palace. Falcon asked the young man to accompany him, and they walked to the center of the great hall, where they could see for a good distance in all directions. The room was dimly lit by low-burning torches, but the illumination was sufficient to reveal that there were no lurkers in the corners to overhear them.

"Claude," Falcon said in a voice that was little more than a whisper, "what do you know of some swarthy-looking warriors coming to visit the Temple within a few days of our departure?"

"Nothing at all," Claude said, puzzled. "Why do you ask?"

As briefly as he could, Falcon explained the events of recent days. Even in the dim light, he could see Claude pale at the knowledge that the Temple was plotting against Philip. He turned even paler when he heard that he was himself under suspicion.

"But this is monstrous!" Claude said, when the recitration was over. "I had thought I was joining a holy order!" He thought for a few minutes, then: "Sir Draco, I now recall something one of the brothers told me. They were pressing me to join the Temple, and telling me tales to impress me with its power. They told of a force of warriors they keep at a castle within the realm of the Greek emperor in or near Anatolia, wherever that is. They said that these men are Turkoman converts, not quite knights but not lay volunteers either. They are supposed to be very fierce and fanatical, quite ready to throw away their lives at the slightest order of the grand master."

"That would fit," Falcon said. "Something like the Assassins commanded by the Old Man of the Mountain at Alamut."

"But," protested Claude, "if they've brought in these fellows to kill Philip, why the boar?"

"That may have been a spur-of-the-moment thing, a chance to do the job quickly and make it seem an accident. It didn't work, and they still have these Easterners."

"We must warn the king," Claude urged.

"He's been warned," Falcon said. "I could urge him to march on the Temple and burn it out like a nest of bandits, but he isn't sure of who's on his side. I think he wants to wait until the try is made, then round up the conspirators."

"That's a dangerous game," Claude said.

"And we're in the middle of it," Falcon commented.

The king's procession wound through the streets that had been old when the city had been called Lutetia and was besieged by Labienus, the lieutenant of Julius Caesar. The king and his courtiers were going to the cathedral of Notre Dame for mass and a ceremony. The escort was uncommonly small. Philip had left most of his guard at the palace, though he was accompanied by his usual pack of cronies, along with Falcon and Wulf, Claude and Isabeau, and Lady Gudrun von Kleist. Also with the group were the grand master of the Temple, accompanied by the knights of the chapter of the Paris Temple.

Falcon, Wulf, and Claude all rode fully armed, Besides Nemesis, his ax, and his dagger, Falcon had his bow and quiver cased on his saddle. At one point during the long, slow procession, the grand master had ridden up beside Falcon.

"You look most warlike for a man on so peaceful a mission," the grand master said.

"I always wear my armor on certain days of the week, no matter where I am. It keeps me accustomed to the weight. I require it of all my soldiers." The grand master nodded and excused himself.

Falcon eyed the crowds that thronged the streets and impeded progress; they were at the windows, even on the rooftops. Danger could lurk in so many places. The crowds waved and cheered, for no reason Falcon could guess except that it was what crowds were expected to do when a king passed.

As they neared the towering cathedral, student robes became more numerous, and Falcon found himself looking for familiar faces. The dark, threatening skies formed an odd contrast to the many colors of the king's retinue. Eventually, the procession emerged from the narrow alleyways into the open square fronting the main doorway of the cathedral.

Falcon felt a tug at the hem of his mail and he looked down. It was Mika "What is it?" he asked.

"Sir Draco!" he shouted, barely heard above the noise of the crowd. "Some of those black-faced rogues were seen today near the cathedral precincts." Falcon spurred his horse, knocking Mika aside. He forced his way toward Philip, who was almost up to the doorway, where a knot of cathedral churchmen awaited him.

Falcon grabbed the king's rein and halted his horse. "No farther, sire. There is danger." Without further ado, Falcon spurred his mount up the steps of the cathedral, scattering monks, priests, and lay brothers. He halted at the line of cathedral officials and demanded: "Have any foreigners arrived here this morning?"

A priest shook a crucifix at him. "Foreigners? What is this outrage? This is the House of God!"

Falcon grabbed a handful of the priest's robe and hauled him up to eye level. "Foreigners, I said, you dolt! Dark men from the East! Tell me quickly if you want to reach the steps alive!"

"Hold!" shouted another priest. "There was a band of pilgrims from Greece who arrived this morning. Now, explain yourself, sir knight!" Falcon dropped the priest.

"Pilgrims? All men? Dark and bearded?"

"Yes."

Falcon wheeled his mount and clattered down the steps straight for Philip. Just as he reached the king he heard a hiss and something punched his shoulder from behind. He threw his arms around Philip and wrestled him from his horse as another arrow glanced from his helmet.

Then the square seemed to be full of dark, armed men. Falcon got Philip against a building with his back to a wall and stood before him, Nemesis clenched in both fists. In an instant, Wulf was beside him, falchion out and buckler in fist. Three men with oddly curved swords rushed them, and Falcon split the first on the upstroke, then brought Nemesis down to cleave the second from crown to waist. Wulf ducked and gutted the third with a backhand sweep of his falchion.

When the arrows had begun to fly, Claude de Coucy had grabbed Isabeau around the waist and lifted her from her saddle. He tossed her down to a crowd of gaping students and shouted: "Take her inside." Then he drew his sword and charged into the brawl. He saw a knot of armed men rush toward the king from a side alley and barreled his horse into the midst of them. He had an impression of black eyes and white teeth in brown faces, then he was dealing skull-splitting strokes on both sides. His horse reared and brained one with its steel-plated forehooves.

"The bastards are all over!" shouted Philip. "Somebody give me a sword!" His demand went unheard in the general confusion. Arrows were still coming from somewhere in the cathedral.

Falcon spotted Mika and his fellow students, who were watching the fun. "You louts make yourselves useful!" he shouted. An assassin rushed him with an ax, and he halved the man at the waist. "You know the cathedral. Go up in the towers and kill those bowmen!" The students drew their swords and rushed to do his bidding.

With blood-curdling howls, five of the Easterners bore down on the king's defenders. Falcon took out the last on the right with a quick diagonal slice, and as he did he dropped to one knee. He brought the blade back in a broad, horizontal cut that caught two more across their midsections. Wulf sliced the neck of the fourth and clouted the fifth in the face with his buckler, driving its center spike up under the cheekbone and into his brain.

"It's getting slippery here, Draco," Wulf said. "We'd better move." The blood and entrails that were collecting had made the footing treacherous, so Falcon and Wulf escorted Philip over to the cathedral steps, their eyes alert for more attackers. The arrows seemed to have stopped coming from the cathedral.

Gudrun came riding up to them, leading Falcon's horse. She held its rein in one hand and his ax in the other. "Get the king mounted and out of here!" she shouted.

"Excellent advice," Falcon said to Philip.

"My people will never see me run from assassins!" Philip shouted.

"If I ever find a reasonable king," Falcon lamented, "I'll swear fealty to him."

Then more assassins appeared from within the cathedral and there was hard work for a while. From the corner of his eye, he saw the little band of Templars siting placidly, awaiting the outcome.

A dark man almost got close enough for a dagger stroke, but Gudrun split him with her ax. Falcon looked around for Wulf but could not see him. Then he was busy with three more of the rogues, who took several seconds to kill.

Then there was a great silence, marred only by occasional groans from the injured. The king was still standing. Falcon saw Wulf and wondered where he'd gotten to, but then he was distracted by Gudrun, who was waving her bloody ax aloft with some Germanic victory cry. Claude de Coucy was riding up and down the cathedral steps, looking for more enemies. Mika and some of the students were emerging from the cathedral, carrying several swarthy heads, which they displayed for the king's admiration.

Then Philip was tapping him on the shoulder. "Come, Sir Draco, I wish to have words with those men." He pointed to the knot of Templars. For a wonder, they were paying no attention to those on the steps. Instead, they were dismounted and clustering around something that lay on the ground.

As Falcon and Philip strode across the square, the crowd set up a great cheering, as if this had all been a spectacle put on just for them. Then they caught sight of the object of the Templars' attention. The grand master lay on the ground, an arrow through his chest. Philip pushed the chapter knights away and bent to examine the shaft.

"A Saracen arrow, you'll notice," he pronounced. "Why, the assassins must have been sent to kill him as well as me, wouldn't you think, Sir Draco?"

"If you say so, sire," Falcon answered. He looked at the chapter knights. They were all as pale as death. "You gentlemen were of damned little help," Falcon said.

"But we were unarmed," protested one. "We had thought we were attending a church service, not a battle."

"How lacking in foresight. You might have found weapons. Even the students defended me."

"You are their king," said another. "Our allegiance is to the Temple."

"I shall remember that," Philip said. "And now, take your master to the Temple for burial. Be glad that you do not accompany him to the grave." Wordlessly, the Templars picked up their dead leader and bore him away. Falcon watched them go.

"Is that all?" Falcon asked. "Aren't you going to arrest the lot and hang them all?"

Philip shook his head. "If only I could. Right now, I need the Temple, Sir Draco. They won't try to kill me again for a while. If I killed everybody who plotted against me I'd have to depopulate half of Europe."

"I'm glad I'm leaving here," Falcon said. "I'll never understand kings or their ways."

"You're a man for a simpler time, Sir Draco," Philip said.

The Archbishop of Paris came down the steps of the cathedral. "We all rejoice in your escape from death, sire," he said. "We shall hold services thanking God for your preservation."

"Yes, no doubt," Philip said. He spotted Claude de Coucy, now dismounted and embracing Isabeau. "You! Claude de Coucy! Come here!" The couple walked to the king and knelt. Philip held his palms out. "Place your hands between mine," he commanded. Claude folded his hands as if in prayer, and Philip clasped them between his own. "For services to your king this day, I, Philip Capet, called Augustus, do confer upon you the fief of Montcalm, to hold at my pleasure and enjoy the fruits and increase thereof, with the title of Baron of Montcalm." He raised Claude to his feet and embraced him. Then he raised Isabeau and embraced her and kissed her on both cheeks. "Consider it a wedding present," Philip said. He looked Isabeau up and down. "Oh, to have the *droit de seigneur* still in force."

"Sire!" said the archbishop, scandalized.

"Silence," Philip said. "I just remembered what I was coming here for." He called to a courtier, and the man handed him a parchment scroll from which hung the royal seal.

"Here is the new royal charter for the cathedral school of Notre Dame. Among other things, it exempts your villainous students from civil law in perpetuity." The students danced and cheered, waving their swords and collected heads.

"And now," Philip said, "Lady Gudrun, if you would do me the honor of riding by my side back to the palace?" Gudrun smiled and nodded. With a lace kerchief she was daintily cleaning the blood from Falcon's ax. The king turned to Falcon. "Sir Draco, please attend me in my privy chamber this evening. You shall not go unrewarded." Falcon bowed and helped Philip to mount.

As the others rode away, Falcon mounted his own horse. Wulf was already in the saddle. Falcon pulled the cover from his quiver and counted arrows. Nineteen. There had been twenty that morning. He looked at Wulf, and the Saxon stared back blandly. He replaced the cover. What was one arrow, anyway? "Let's go gather our things," he said to Wulf. "I want to see the last of this place."

Outside the great gate of Paris, five riders gathered in the morning mist. Claude and Isabeau were taking their leave of the others. "Yet again I thank you, Sir Draco, both for rescuing Claude from the Temple and for placing him in the way of royal favor."

"The first was a favor," Falcon said. "I'm not sure the second was. Go now, you two. Life is too short to waste on gôodbyes." The two turned and rode, to be joined by Isabeau's servants.

"Sir Draco," said Gudrun, "I return to Germany now. Should your steps lead you there, you know that my castle gate always stands open to you."

"Be assured, lady, that I shall not miss the opportunity." Mentally, he made a vow never to let any space smaller than a good-sized county come between himself and her demesne.

As Falcon and Wulf took their road back to their winter quarters, a pleasant jingling came from their saddlebags. "Five hundred gold florins," said Falcon complacently. "Not a bad haul for a few days of drinking and eating and tourneying."

"Not to mention twenty from Benedetto," commented Wulf.

"And ten from Gudrun," Falcon said.

"Do me one favor, though, my lord," Wulf said.

"What's that?"

"Never mention Aristotle to me again."

"Never. I promise." Predictably, it started to rain.

The following is an action-packed
excerpt from the next novel in this
sword-swinging new Signet series
set in the age of chivalry:
THE FALCON #4
THE KING'S TREASURE

The long column of mounted men snaked its way down
the side of the ravine and into the mist. The ravine was a
singularly evil-looking place. Dark, tangled foliage over-
hung the bank and matted bracken grew down the sides.
The bottom of the ravine was obscured in fog. The path
was so narrow that the horses had to place each hoof
directly before the other, and the wagons were in imminent danger of tumbling into the gorge. A potbellied,
one-eyed old man walked ahead of the wagons and directed their drivers as they inched their way down the
path. Most of the old man's words involved some kind of
blasphemy or obscenity.

A few hundred paces down the path widened and two
men rode side by side. One was hideously ugly, with a
face so scarred by sword cuts that it seemed to be made
up of the ill-matched parts of several faces. One of his
ears was missing. The other man was younger and sandy-
haired, and at his saddle he carried a morningster: a spiked
ball attached to a wooden handle by two feet of chain.

"Where's Draco and Wulf?" asked the ugly one. His
name was Donal MacFergus and he had an ax ready at his
own saddle. Both men wore shirts of mail and helmets.

"They must be ahead of us, farther down," said the
other. He was called Simon the Monk because he had
spent several years in a monastery before becoming a
soldier. "They started down ahead of us, and there's no
way we could have passed them on that path."

"I don't know," said Donal uneasily, as he looked about
him. The fog was now too dense to penetrate more than

a few feet. "Strange things happen in fog. Spirits move about in fog that fear the daylight. They can trick you."

"Oh, cease your prattle of spirits," said the other uncomfortably. "This isn't Ireland, you know." All the same, Simon's eyes were a little wider as he scanned the fog.

Down in the densest and darkest of the mist, two more riders led the procession. They inched along, their mounts feeling a slow way down toward the sound of running water. Thick ropes and skeins of fog twisted and swirled around them like a basket of writhing serpents.

"Have you ever seen such stuff?" asked the one with yellow hair spilling out from under his helmet. "By Jesus, if the Devil were a spider, this would be his cobweb!"

The other said nothing, but he kept turning his head from side to side. From his conical helmet a steel nasal slanted down to protect his nose, and from either side of the nasal his flint-gray eyes stared fixedly. The eyes were all that was visible of his face, for the rest was hidden beneath a veil of iron mesh. The veil continued downward to join a long coat of mail that dropped below the rider's knees. It had long, tightly fitted sleeves to the wrists, and his hands were covered with thick black leather gloves which were studded on their backs with short iron spikes.

His name was Draco Falcon. He was owner, captain, and lord of this little army of some two hundred men, which he now feared to be hopelessly lost. While one hand held his rein, the other rested on the hilt of a long, curved sword which hung at his belt. He thought he saw a shadow flit in the mist below.

"What was that?" said the yellow-haired man.

"I don't know," Falcon said, "but I saw it, too."

The younger man loosened the short sword at his waist. His name was Wulf, which was short for Aethelwulf Ecgbehrtsson. His sword was short, broad, and curved, and a small shield was hung from its scabbard. He wore a short, sleeveless vest of mail in addition to his steel cap. He hated fog as much as anyone.

"Grendel used to walk in the fog," Wulf said. "He'd sneak up to the hall at Heorot and break in the doors and snatch up the sleeping thegns. He'd bite their heads off and hold their carcasses over his head like wineskins while he drank their blood."

"I'm more worried about men than about monsters," Falcon said. "I've been a soldier long enough to know a fine ambush site when I see one." His voice was slightly muffled by the cloth-lined veil of mail over his mouth.

There were more of the flitting shadows. Were they men? What else would they be. He had traveled more than most men, and had always been assured, wherever he went, that nearby there were giants, fabulous beasts, werewolves, vampires, or the like. Nevertheless, in spite of all these assurances, he had never encountered a single example of the supernatural.

"If they're men," Wulf said, "they'll know better than to attack a force the size of ours."

"How are they to know how many of us there are?" Falcon asked. "If they see only two men, they'll probably attack." Neither assumed that the men might be friendly. Nobody lurked in fog with good intentions. In any case, strangers were always assumed to be hostile until proven otherwise.

There were noises now that did not seem to be caused by the river that flowed sluggishly at the bottom of the ravine. There was a clatter of rocks and an unmistakable clink of metal. "Get ready," Falcon muttered. He reached down and freed his long, kite-shaped shield from its place at his saddle. His left forearm went through its straps, and he tightened them until he was satisfied with the shield's fit.

"Keep your back toward the bank," Falcon advised. It would help keep most of the enemy in front, if it came to a fight. The path had now debouched onto a narrow bench of land between the river and the slope of the ravine. The water shone black as old blood. The growth along its bank was thick but sickly-looking, and no trace of froth marked its surface.

"This looks like a dragon's lair," Wulf said, "a haunt for orcs and nixies and nicors."

"Keep your mind on more dangerous things," Falcon said. "I've not encountered a dragon yet, but men are another matter. Let's wait here until the rest of the men—" The first rock clanged from his helmet. Falcon jerked his shield up to protect his face. The mail would keep him from being cut, but a rock could still smash bones through the flexible armor.

Wulf cursed as a stone struck his thigh. He jumped from his horse and darted into the fog. The horse stayed where it was, afraid to move in the obscuring mist. A rock struck Falcon's horse on the neck and it reared. As soon as he had the beast under control, Falcon dismounted. Trying to fight mounted was futile under such circumstances. Shield held high, Falcon stood with his back to the bank, awaiting his enemies. He did not have long to wait.

A few more stones rattled off his shield, then the hidden men attacked. He had an impression of long, unkempt hair, swirling beards, snarling teeth, and ragged clothes. One swung at him with a heavy wooden club, but Falcon took him out of action with a short cut to the wrist. The man howled and dropped his club. Falcon's long, curved sword was meant to be used with both hands, but it was possible to utilize it single-handed as long as really powerful blows were not necessary. Another man charged with a stone tied to a stick. Falcon cut the man's thigh and he beat a limping retreat. As long as the attackers were as poorly armed and unarmored as this, he should have no difficulty in holding out until his men arrived.

Then the others confronted him. They were big men in full mail, and there were at least six of them. They loomed in the fog like giants. Falcon released the handhold of his shield and slipped his forearm from the forearm strap. He let the shield dangle from his shoulder by the guige strap. This way, it afforded his left side some protection while he used the sword with both hands.

The first to the attack wore a long hauberk of mail and a flat-topped helmet with a nasal. His shield was small and oval and it bore no device. This man was a good deal more of an opponent than the first ones. He bore a sword, long and straight. The blade was notched, but Falcon knew that it could cut grievously nonetheless. The wielder essayed an overhand cut at the helm to draw the shield upward, but Falcon did not respond. In the midst of the stroke, the mailed man cut low, to sever the knee tendon. Falcon merely dipped his shoulder, and the long point of the shield intercepted the blade.

The frustrated warrior tried a high cut at the neck, but

by that time Falcon had picked his point of aim and brought the broad, curved blade up and into the armpit of his enemy's hauberk, where the intricate tailoring of the mail links made a weak spot. The unusual blade split the opposing rings and cut into the muscles and nerves of his enemy. The sword dropped, the man screamed, and Falcon wheeled to face the rest of his opponents.

There were too many of them. Some wore the long mail hauberks of knights: knee-length with sleeves to the wrist or elbow. They had mail covering their heads and helmets with nasal bars. None wore the face-covering helms that were now popular but which restricted hearing and sight.

A man roared and charged. He held his shield high and Falcon dropped and slashed low, carving a leg from under the man. There was a bitten-off grunt as the man fell. Then another warrior was there, his spear held at a menacing angle. Falcon backed toward the cliff. He knew from long, hard experience that a man with a spear could be far more dangerous than any swordsman. The man feinted high, and Falcon flexed his shoulder to take the point. The spearman raised his point and went in over the shield at the neck.

Falcon dropped to the ground. This man was deadly. His opponent stabbed at him repeatedly, but Falcon drew as much of himself as he could beneath his shield. He made a small cut to the ankle. His opponent skipped back at the last possible instant. Another came in swinging with a mace. Falcon brought the curved sword across horizontally at waist level. It did not split the man's mail, but the blow was powerful enough to drop him, retching. The spearman took advantage of the distraction to try another attack.

Falcon struck the spear point upward with the crescent hilt of his sword, then brought the blade across and down in an oblique cut that split the spearman from shoulder to waist.

Wulf was stumbling about in the fog. His small shield was insufficient to protect him from the flying rocks, so he sought to close with his enemies and deal with them using his falchion. The short, curved blade was ideal for this sort of close-quarter fighting, but the damned fog was so confusing that he was unsure in which direction to charge. Two ragged attackers appeared and he ducked beneath their crude weapons and gutted the two of them with a single horizontal stroke. Then there was a man in armor who wore a face-covering helm, and he had an ax. Wulf dove for the ground. He heard the ax whistle over his head and he got his feet beneath him and sprang to his full height, bringing the blade up between the other man's legs and splitting him to the navel.

Another rock bounced off his steel cap. He was ready to howl with frustration. Where were the rest of the men? Another enemy appeared before him. This one wore a long hauberk and mail hose and a face-covering helm. He gripped a long sword in both hands. This could be tricky. A man so completely armored had few weak spots. Wulf got his back as close as possible to the steep bank so that he could devote his full attention to dealing with the knight.

The armored man came in swinging, and at that moment Wulf knew that this was no knight. The man was obviously unused to the weight of his armor, and he did not allow for the sag and sway of the iron fabric, which shifted the wearer's center of balance. The man tried a blow which should have taken Wulf's head off, but the blow missed by several inches.

Wulf timed his move carefully and ducked beneath the next blow, coming up behind his enemy and swinging his blade. There was no sense in dulling his edge against the heavy mail, so he cracked the man across the shoulders with the flat. The mailed bandit whirled clumsily, and Wulf danced back. The armored man burst into an oxlike charge, sword held high for a stroke calculated to split Wulf from crown to crotch. At the last possible instant, Wulf danced nimbly aside and let the man lumber past, giving him a boot in his mailed backside for further impetus. The man took several lurching steps and saw that he was headed straight for the riverbank. He tried to halt himself, but he had built up too much momentum in his heavy mail. He tottered for a horror-stricken moment, then fell into the water with a tremendous splash. He sank in his iron like a kettle full of bricks.

Wulf ran for the bank, and three more of the ragged

men tried to block him. He cursed and turned, running back along the level ground to where he could hear the sounds of Falcon dealing with his attackers.

Donal and Simon heard the sounds of battle long before they could do anything about it. They cursed the treacherous path that restrained them to a slow walk. It was clear from the sounds that their companions were battling outrageously superior numbers. They knew that they faced the disgrace of feudal soldiers who allowed their masters to be killed without aiding them. Simon called back up the line of men that there was fighting ahead, and he could hear the clatter of weapons being readied.

They found themselves at the bottom. "Where are you, my lord?" Donal called through trumpeted hands. Then he saw the familiar, shaggy form of Wulf darting from one wall of fog to another. "This way," he cried, and they followed him into the obscurity. Donal had his ax in his hand, its wrist thong securing it. Behind him, he heard the rhythmic clicking of Simon's morningstar as the exmonk whirled the spiked ball in circles around the haft. This kept the swing of the ball under his control. It also confused the enemy as to where the attack would come from.

They burst upon the scene of the action just as some twenty bandits were closing in upon the two beleagured men, who now stood back-to-back, menacing the encircling bandits with their stained weapons. The two horsemen split, Donal to the left and Simon to the right, plying their weapons to both sides, lopping limbs and scattering brains with each stroke. The bandits milled about uncertainly. Then a group of horsemen and footmen arrived, howling and striking, and the bandits broke and fled.

Falcon and Wulf stood, breathing heavily, while the men mopped up. "Watch yourselves!" Falcon shouted. "They'll hide in this damned fog and try to pick you off!" The men stayed together in small bands as they scoured the riverbank in both directions. They dragged the bodies back to where Falcon stood for systematic looting. No man tried ot take anything for himself, for Falcon's discipline was strict and expulsion from the band was the punishment for witholding loot.

The gloom of the gorge began to lighten as the late-morning sun burned away the fog. In the light, the fearsome attackers presented a less intimidating appearance. Most were filthy men in rags, no more than serfs who had armed themselves with any makeshift weapon they could. The armored men were either degraded knights or peasants who had stolen their gear from ambushed warriors. The mail was rusty, the helms dented and in poor repair, even the swords were rusted and stained, any gold or jewels once inlaid on their hilts long since gouged out.

Nevertheless, iron was valuable and always in short supply. The mail could be cleaned and refurbished by tumbling in a barrel with gravel, sand, and vinegar. Even the broken weapons and split helms could be sold to smiths as scrap. Wulf led a party to where the heavily armored man had fallen into the water, and they prodded with spear shafts until they located him, then dragged the corpse ashore.

Falcon's men were experienced and efficient, and when they were finished only the most verminous rags and hides were left with the bodies. As a final touch, Donal went among the corpses, methodically hacking the heads off with his ax. He piled the heads in a neat pyramid. He had long since explained to Falcon that this was an ancient Irish custom and it was supposed to placate some spirits or ancestors or some such. In any case, it would serve as a salutary warning to the next band of outlaws to use this as an ambush spot.

When all the loot was packed away and the wagon's safely down from the gorge path, Falcon ordered the men to remount. Unlike most armies of the time, Falcon's was entirely mounted. Even the men who fought on foot rode into action. Falcon believed in mobility. For the same reason, he did not tolerate the usual train of camp followers that slowed most armies to a crawl.

They rode downstream for most of the day. Gradually, the river valley widened until they were riding in a broad, pleasant river bottom with grassy meadows, which were probably fine pasture in the spring but which were now deserted with the onset of winter. The grass was close-cropped from last summer's pasturage, and brown from the advancing year.

Falcon looked up at the sky. It was darkening again, this time with high, fluff-bottomed clouds that portended snow.

"How long till the Feast of Nativity?" Falcon asked Simon, who rode beside him. The ex-monk counted laboriously on his fingers.

"Four weeks and odd days," Simon said.

"Then we're in for an early snow," Falcon said, gazing upward. Just their luck to be caught in a heavy snow in the mountain valleys. It was more than an inconvenience. It could be deadly.

Once again, Falcon questioned his wisdom in accepting this commission. He was to escort a treasure from Limoges to Cahors, across the Auvergne Mountains, in winter. King Richard of England had died trying to wrest the treasure from the Viscount of Limoges. The mission was to be kept a strict secret, of course, but Falcon knew how difficult it was to keep secrets where treasure was concerned.

The viscount was a suspicious man. He had agreed to the contract Falcon proposed, but he was not keeping the treasure in Limoges. Instead, it was in a small castle here in Limousin. The castle was on land that the viscount claimed, but the land was now technically English territory. Since the new King John of England was a monarch of little account, this borderland belonged to any who could hold it. Under heavy secrecy, the viscount had sent the treasure to this castle, which had been built by an ancestor and had been deserted for a generation or more. Falcon had been directed to take this unlikely route to the castle, once more for reasons of secrecy.

By the end of the day, they had the castle in sight. One look told Falcon why it had been abandoned for so long. It was of a very antiquated design: a single stone-and-timber tower surrounded by a circular earthenwork rampart. The rampart had once been topped by a timber palisade, but the logs had long since been scavenged. A man standing atop the tower blew a trumpet, and several men issued from the interior. They mounted and rode out to meet the newcomers.

Falcon signaled for his standard-bearer to unfurl the banner. The big Spanish knight who had that duty complied, and the Falcon banner flapped in the chill wind. Against a background stitched with silver thread, it depicted a black falcon with wings spread. In its talons, the falcon gripped blue lightning bolts.

Ahead of the other horsemen from the castle rode a tall, bearded man in mail of good quality. His coif was down and he wore no helm, but it hung ready at his saddle. In this disputed territory, a man was best advised to be cautious. He halted a few paces from Falcon.

"You would be Sir Draco Falcon, I take it?" the man said.

"I'm Falcon."

"Good. We've been expecting you the last few days. I'm Sir Rauf de Chaluz. Come with me to the castle. We've gotten some sheep and pigs and a few fowl from the local peasants. At least we can offer you a decent meal before you set out in the morning."

"Excellent," Falcon said. "We've been living on cheese and hard bread and salted fish for days." The prospect of real food was cheering.

They rode through the gateless gap in the rampart and into the bailey: the open field between the rampart and the tower. In the bailey, servants were bustling, slaughtering the livestock for dinner. Falcon directed his men to pitch their tents, for the tower was far too small to hold them all. The standard-bearer, Ruy Ortiz, began posting sentries on the rampart.

"The land's in dispute, but we're not at war," Sir Rauf said. "I keep a man on watch up in the tower. Sentries aren't necessary."

"My men are always under wartime discipline," Falcon answered. "We always post sentries, and the men stay under arms."

Wulf came to take Falcon's horse and Sir Rauf led him up the artificial mound atop which the castle stood. A short flight of steps led up the wall to a landing on the second story. The castle had no openings at ground level. A wooden bridge crossed from the landing to another ten feet away. From the second landing, a low door allowed entrance to the tower. Under attack, the bridge could be drawn up, leaving no access to the tower. The bridge smelled of freshcut wood. Rauf's men must have replaced it when they arrived.

The inside of the tower was pitch-black. At Rauf's call a man appeared on a flight of steps with a torch, and by its smoky light Rauf led Falcon up and into a large room which had once been the castle's great hall. In a castle, the walls got thinner as one went higher, so the largest rooms were always on the upper floors.

In the room, Falcon could see several strong chests, all locked and the keyholes covered with lead. The lead was impressed with the viscount's seal. "Any idea what's in the chests?" Falcon asked.

Sir Rauf shook his head. "None. Only the viscount and his most trusted henchmen know. Rumors are rife, though."

"They always are," Falcon observed. "What do these rumors say?"

"Some hold that it's an old Viking hoard. Others say it's a pagan idol of solid gold. You know how men talk. Whatever it is, I'll be damned glad to get it off my hands."

"I can't blame you," Falcon said. "Has absolute secrecy been maintained?"

"As far as I know. The men I've brought here know, of course, but they're absolutely trustworthy. Even so, I'm to keep them here for a week after you've left."

Falcon grunted. He'd lost count of the "absolutely trustworthy" men he'd known who had turned traitor.

"Come upstairs for some wine," Sir Rauf invited. Falcon followed the knight up the stairs and into another room. This one was well lighted because it had originally had a wooden roof which was now gone. About half of the roof had been replaced, and a section of the roofed-over area was screened off with tenting. Several men were gathered around an improvised hearth where a fire burned and wine was being heated. One of the men poured a cup of the mulled wine and handed it to Falcon. The man wore a priest's plain cassock. He was big and he walked heavily, although he did not seem fat. He made a slight clicking noise as he walked, and Falcon glanced down to see mail-clad feet strapped with spurs of plain steel.

"This is Bishop LaCru. He will be accompanying you to oversee the papal tithe."

"Nobody said anything about a churchman being along," Falcon protested.

"Nevertheless, he must go," Rauf said.

"I assure you, Sir Draco," LaCru said, "I shall not be a burden or a hindrance." Falcon shrugged. At least the man looked as if he could take care of himself.

There was a stirring from the curtained-off section, and someone came through the cloth. It was a woman. Her face, framed by coif and wimple, was undeniably beautiful, with straight, haughty features and black, level brows. She was small, but the tight fit of her gown revealed a full figure. She gazed at Falcon with large brown eyes.

"This is Lady Constance," Sir Rauf announced. "She is the viscount's niece. She will be going along with you also."

About the Author

MARK RAMSAY was born on St. John's Day, 1947. He is a professional writer and he lives on a remote mountaintop in the Appalachian Mountains. When not writing, he pursues his lifelong study of the Medieval and Classical periods. He makes his own weapons and armor and sometimes fights with them, when he can find someone to practice with. He feels this brings a breath of authenticity to his writing.

JOIN <u>THE FALCON</u> READER'S PANEL AND PREVIEW NEW BOOKS

If you're a reader of <u>THE FALCON</u>, New American Library wants to bring you more of the type of books you enjoy. For this reason we're asking you to join <u>THE FALCON</u> Reader's Panel, to preview new books, so we can learn more about your reading tastes.

Please fill out and mail this questionnaire today. Your comments are appreciated.

1. The title of the last paperback book I bought was:
   TITLE:_____PUBLISHER:_____

2. How many paperback books have you bought for yourself in the last six months?
   ☐ 1 to 3   ☐ 4 to 6   ☐ 7 to 9   ☐ 10 to 20   ☐ 21 or more

3. What other paperback fiction have you read in the past six months? Please list titles:_____
   _____
   _____
   _____

4. My favorite is (one of the above or other):_____

5. My favorite author is:_____

6. I watch television, on average (check one):
   ☐ Over 4 hours a day   ☐ 2 to 4 hours a day   ☐ 0 to 2 hours a day
   I usually watch television (check one or more):
   ☐ 8 a.m. to 5 p.m.   ☐ 5 p.m. to 11 p.m.   ☐ 11 p.m. to 2 a.m.

7. I read the following numbers of different magazines regularly (check one):
   ☐ More than 6   ☐ 3 to 6 magazines   ☐ 0 to 2 magazines
   My favorite magazines are:_____
   _____

For our records, we need this information from all our Reader's Panel Members.

NAME:_____
ADDRESS:_____
CITY:_____STATE:_____ZIP CODE:_____
TELEPHONE: Area Code ( ) Number_____

8. (Check one) ☐ Male   ☐ Female

9. Age (check one): ☐ 17 and under   ☐ 18 to 34   ☐ 35 to 49
   ☐ 50 to 64   ☐ 65 and over

10. Education (check one):
    ☐ Now in high school   ☐ Graduated high school
    ☐ Now in college   ☐ Completed some college
    ☐ Graduated college

11. What is your occupation? (check one):
    ☐ Employed full-time   ☐ Employed part-time   ☐ Not employed
    Give your full job title:_____

Thank you. Please mail this today to:

THE FALCON, New American Library,
1633 Broadway, New York, New York 10019